MURMURS OF THE DEVIL

DESIRED BY THE DEVIL

BOOK THREE

BELLA MOONDRAGON

Cover by Sparrow Book Cover Designs

❋ Created with Vellum

For Kody

For Kody

CONTENTS

1

EYES ON ME

Julia

I swear there's somebody watching me.

The fine hairs on the back of my neck prickle to life as a deep sense of unease slinks across my skin. It's not a new feeling, not here in this huge house on the edge of the swamp, but it still hits me hard every time, drawing the air from my lungs and sending hot fear careening through my veins.

But when I whip around to glance at the doorway of the bedroom, there's nobody there.

There never is.

"Julia?" My best friend's voice filters through my phone's speakers, grounding me back in reality. "Are you still there?" Nina asks, concern leaking into her normally peppy tone.

"Mhm," I hum, my eyes still fixed on the empty threshold.

"You sound so distracted," Nina continues. "I thought you said you were bored out of your mind?"

"Oh, I am," I confirm. "There's nothing at all to do in Hahnville, unless you like quilting blankets for alligators or whatever it is the women do out here."

Nina tries and fails to hold back a snort. "So it's safe to say you haven't made any new friends? At least you have Jake all to yourself out there. That must be quite the change from New York."

Any eeriness I felt earlier is overtaken by exasperation as soon as she mention's my husband's name. "It would be great, if he was actually home for more than a day or two at a time."

Nina pauses for a moment before she responds. All of her teasing cheerfulness is gone when she probes, "Jules, you don't think he's… you know, seeing somebody again?"

My gaze flickers to the ensuite bathroom door. Jake had gone in there a few minutes before, saying he had to take a shower before leaving for yet another business trip. The burble of running water filters out into the bedroom, but I don't trust it to mask the sound of our conversation entirely.

Not wanting to risk it, I creep out of the bedroom and into the hallway. "Don't even start this again, Nina," I warn in a low voice.

"He's gone all the time," Nina points out. "And from what you describe, your sex life is about as exciting as waiting in line at the DMV."

I head down the stairs toward the kitchen as I argue, "Yes, but that doesn't automatically mean he's cheating. He just works hard. Jake sunk a ton of money into this house, and it had to come from somewhere. Besides, you wouldn't believe how much they're charging us to remove that ghastly cemetery from the swamp."

As I hoped, Nina latches on to this new piece of information. "Finally!" she exclaims. "Those pictures you sent made it look like you were living in Dracula's fucking castle. Good riddance!"

I emerge into the kitchen and make a beeline for the fancy espresso machine on the counter. I had it imported straight from Italy and never once regretted the hassle of getting it through customs. Prepping the grounds, I reply, "Honestly, it's so creepy. Just the thought of all of those bodies rotting away in practically my backyard, it makes my skin crawl."

"I mean, who would actually want to be buried out there?"

"The people from the historical society said it's an ancestral graveyard," I explain. "I guess that before us, the property was owned by a single family. Whenever they died, they'd just bury them in the swamp."

"Gross," Nina replies. "That feels like a perfect way to be haunted by your great-great-grandma forever."

Whatever presence I've been feeling out here, something tells me it's not somebody's elderly grandparent. But I'm certainly not going to tell Nina about the weird stuff that's been going on in the house since we moved in. While she is my best friend, she's not exactly known for her discretion. If I said something to her about it now, half of our social circle would think that I'm hysterical over some spooky graveyard by this time tomorrow.

And that's why I feel the need to reply sternly, "Nina, there's no such thing as ghosts."

I can practically hear her roll her eyes over the phone as I gather up my freshly brewed latte and start toward the living room. "Haunted or not, it's still fucking weird," she insists, and I can't help but agree with her.

Just as I step out into the hallway and open my mouth to reply, a colossal bang echoes through the kitchen behind me. A startled cry stutters in my throat as I jump at the sudden sound. Hot coffee sloshes over the side of the mug I'm holding, splattering onto the pristine hardwood floor.

"What the fuck was that?" Nina asks sharply. "Jules? Jules, are you okay?"

Am I?

I turn around to face the kitchen doorway and decide that I am definitely not okay.

Seconds before, the room had been neat and tidy, everything in order.

But now, every single cabinet door is standing open, swaying slightly on their hinges as though rocked by some spectral breeze.

"I... I'm fine," I choke out, unable to tear my gaze from the unexplainable scene as adrenaline hurtles through my veins.

"What the hell happened?"

"Something fell," I lie, eyeing the cabinets with a mix of fear and suspicion. "And I spilled my coffee. I've got to go and get this cleaned up."

I can tell that Nina doesn't quite buy my story, but she doesn't argue. Instead, we exchange our goodbyes and end the call. Placing my phone and the half empty mug on the kitchen counter, I run my hand over the cabinet doors, swinging them shut until the last one closes with a gentle click. I glare at them for a moment, daring them to open again, but they remain innocently motionless under my watchful stare.

Finally, when my eyes start to water, and I begin to feel stupid at letting a breeze and some cabinets rattle me so badly, I turn away. Gathering up a fistful of paper towels, I turn my attention to the spill.

Coffee pools on the hardwood, flowing between the cracks in muddy little rivers. It's a tragic scene. I drop the paper towels on top of the liquid and use the sole of my designer heel to push it around. I'm just bending down to retrieve the sodden paper when Jake appears at the other end of the hallway.

"Great view, honey," he grins. "What are you doing?"

"I spilled something," I explain, unable to keep the fear from seeping into my voice. "I made myself a cup of coffee, but when I went to leave the room, all of the cabinets flew open. Isn't that weird?"

Jake laughs and shakes his head, dismissing my unease. "Julia, we've talked about this. This is a new house, and it's built on soft ground. Everything is just settling."

"It's creepy," I huff, crossing my arms over my chest. "I hate it here, Jake. I really do. Stuff like this happens all the time, and I always feel like I'm being watched, like something doesn't want me here."

Jake sighs dramatically, as though I'm making a huge deal out of nothing. "It's just your mind playing tricks on you, Julia. You're lonely and bored, and your brain is messing with you."

"I'm only lonely and bored because you're never here," I shoot back.

"Honey, you know I'd rather be here with you," he soothes, trying to reassure me. He wraps an arm around my waist, pulling me into his side. "But I'm so close to closing on this huge deal, and I'm meeting with investors this week to get this thing off the ground. Once I get it in the bag, I'll be all yours."

He guides me toward the front door, where his duffel bag and briefcase are waiting. Once he releases me in favor of his luggage, I follow him as he opens the door and steps out into the sweltering summer heat.

As the afternoon humidity chases away the coolness of the house's air conditioning from my skin, I'm reminded of yet another reason why I despise living here. It's practically tropical. The heat curls around the trunks of the cypress trees that line the shaded drive in a greenish haze. The sky is heavy with purplish, brooding clouds that look ready to burst. I really hope it doesn't storm tonight, not when I'm home alone.

One of Jake's bright red sports cars is parked outside behind the contractor's trucks, pitting the vehicles in stark contrast. I watch as my husband tosses his bags into the back seat before he returns to where I linger on the doorstop.

"You'll be fine, Julia," he assures me. "I'll only be gone for a little while."

"I know," I sigh. As much as he gets on my nerves sometimes, I really don't want Jake to leave me here, but there isn't much I can do about that.

"Bye, honey." He leans in, and my heart thunders as I expect him to catch my lips in a heated kiss, but he simply presses his mouth chastely against mine before pulling away.

Disappointment wells in my chest as Jake retreats to the car, opens the driver's side door, and slips behind the wheel. Seconds later, he's revving down the driveway, and then he's gone.

Solitude settles over me as I stand in the doorway. I'm about to go back inside when voices drift over from the side of the house, growing closer. Two men appear, carrying a mossy, gray chunk of stone between them. As they approach, I realize with heightening apprehension that it's a grave marker..

"Howdy, ma'am," one worker greets me as he catches sight of me standing there.

"Hi," I offer back. "Any problems out there?"

"No, Mrs. Carter," the second guy replies. "We've just got another stone up. Want to take a look?"

I don't particularly want to, but morbid curiosity compels me to nod. The men tilt the stone so that I can see the inscription. The whole thing is overrun by lichen and the edges of the letters are softened by time, but I can decipher enough of the date to realize that whoever this grave belonged to had only been alive for six years.

"A child?" I gasp. I don't know why I should be so surprised. It used to be common for kids to die young from things like fevers or consumption. But when a second set of men round the corner of the house with a decaying wooden box held between them, a second wave of shock hits me. The coffin, for that's what it surely is, is so *small*.

"You never get used to it," the first of the contractors calls from where he and his colleague are loading the gravestone onto the bed of the nearest truck.

"Do you do this a lot? Moving graves, I mean," I ask, grateful to drag my attention away from the tiny coffin.

"It ain't our first rodeo, ma'am," he explains. "There's all sorts of protocols to follow, so there are only a few companies that'll do it. But we're making good progress here. Look, here's the first stone we pulled up today."

He and his partner hold up another grave marker, this one flat and not nearly as faded.

"Hezekiah James," I read.

And as I say the name out loud, I'm once again sure that I can feel eyes on me.

Only this time, I don't turn around to look.

2
SIDE PIECE

Jake

"I missed you, Jake."

The woman's words linger on the humid night air.

What's her name again? Ellie something, I think. She's a busty blonde that I'd picked up at a real estate development conference a few months earlier. After spending several raucous nights in the hotel room with her, coupled with the fact that she lives in New Orleans, she's currently my most convenient option for a quick and willing fuck.

She isn't the only one, of course. I've got women scattered across the country, and they tend to make themselves available to me once they know I'll be in town on business. But with most of my meetings scheduled for the New Orleans office, I've been seeing a lot more of Ellie lately.

"I missed you too," I fib. The whole truth is that sometimes I find myself daydreaming wistfully about the feeling of my cock in her cunt, but her personality is utterly forgettable.

I raise my arms above my head and allow myself a luxurious stretch before settling back down onto the sheets. The silky fabric clings to my sweat-soaked limbs, a reminder of the way I'd pumped my lust and frustration out into Ellie's compliant body. The smell of sex, heavy and cloying, hangs in the stifling air.

"Don't you have AC?" I ask her, kicking the sheets away from my overheated skin.

Ellie shakes her head. "The window unit's busted."

Just my luck. When I'd told her that I'd wanted a steamy night at her place, I hadn't meant it quite so literally. It's hotter than hell in here.

I suddenly find myself longing for the state of the art HVAC system that pumps immaculately cool air through the house I had built on the edge of the swamp. Honestly, it's one of the only things about the place that I actually like. When I'm inside, I can pretend that I'm still in New York and not camped out in the ass crack of nowhere. That is, if some weird shit isn't going down in the house.

Goosebumps creep across my skin as I consider some of the unusual experiences that I've endured in the new house. Even though I've told Julia that it's just the house settling, or the pipes, or whatever bullshit I conjure up in the moment, I can't help but think that there is something there, something strange and unexplainable.

Doors open and close on their own. Objects never seem to stay in their proper places. A few times, I've sworn that Julia was thumping around upstairs in those hideous designer heels of hers, but when I've checked, she's always been out shopping and spending all of my hard earned cash.

And don't even get me started on that fucking swamp. The smell alone is bad enough, but that cemetery really takes the cake. Every time I look out there, I feel like I'm going to see the Creature from the Black Lagoon rise up out of the mud.

But it's almost worse when I don't look. For some reason, I can't shake the sensation that there's something standing out beneath the gnarled trunks of the cypress trees, staring.

Watching.

Waiting.

The thought makes me shiver in spite of the oppressive heat. I'm not scared, though. There's nothing out there, not really. It's just some stupid trick of the mind brought on by Julia's incessant nagging and the weird way that the light shifts out over the marsh.

"Jake, are you okay?" Ellie frowns, running her small hands down my arms. "You look like somebody just walked over your grave."

I choke out a strangled laugh as an image of that grotesque cemetery in the middle of the swamp flashes through my mind. "I'm fine," I manage.

Ellie opens her pretty bow mouth to say something, but she doesn't get a chance. My phone startles to life, ringing and lighting up cheerfully to reveal a picture of me and Julia, one that I'd drunkenly snapped at a party back in New York before we'd moved.

Grateful for the distraction, I snatch up the device and hit the green button to accept the call. I hold one finger out to a pouting Ellie, shushing her as I say into the speaker, "Hello?"

"Howdy Jake, it's Thurman," a familiar voice greets in a heavy Texas drawl.

"What's up?" I ask. I can never tell with Thurman. His tone never seems to change, regardless of whether he's giving me good news or bad.

"Just wanted to let you know that the latest shipment came in with no problems," the man says slowly.

I glance over at Ellie, who's watching me curiously. Damn. The last thing I need is for one of my side pieces to catch wind of what I'm doing and try to hold that over me, so I choose my next words very carefully when I ask, "And the, uh, produce? It's all there?"

"Yup," Thurman confirms. "Everybody's accounted for. We should be all set for the first construction site next week."

"Music to my ears, Thurman," I grin. "Thanks."

"No problem, boss," he replies in that same unaffected tone. "Any luck with the investors?"

"I'm pretty sure we'll have them in the bag after this week. In a few short days, Carter Real Estate Developers will officially become Carter Real Estate Developers and Construction," I assure him. "We'll be fully funded and fully staffed."

"Good to hear," Thurman responds.

There really isn't much more to say, especially with Ellie's impatient hands beginning to roam over my body. I wrap the call up quickly as she adds more incentive by way of trailing a line of hot kisses down my neck.

As soon as I hang up, Ellie's blue eyes widen, and she asks, "Are you really here on business, or just to see me?"

"Who says you aren't business, baby?" I tease as I curl a lock of her bottle blonde hair around one of my fingers.

Ellie rolls her eyes, but smiles all the same. "I mean, which is the excuse to get out of Dodge? Me or these mysterious business deals of yours?"

"You, of course," I grin. "But I really am here on business too. I'm expanding my company, which means meeting with investors. It's not my fault that they happen to be based right here in New Orleans, same as you."

"You're gone so much, your wife is going to hate you," Ellie jabs. Do I detect a little jealousy leaching into her tone? That makes things a bit more interesting. Maybe I've been underestimating just how entertaining she can be.

"I think she already does." I consider how Julia always seems to find fault in everything I do. Apparently, it's not enough that I work my ass off to shower her in money and expensive gifts. Hell, I even built a whole fucking house for her. I glance around Ellie's cramped apartment, with its yellowed walls, sagging ceiling, and no goddamn AC. Julia should be grateful, but it never seems to be enough for her.

Maybe it never will be.

"Is that why you travel so often?" the blonde woman presses. "To get away from her?"

"Not exactly," I hedge.

If I really wanted to escape from Julia's vexing clutches, I'd divorce her. Even in New York after she'd found out about one of my little indiscretions, and we'd fought viciously, I'd stayed with her.

"Then why?"

I close my eyes and let out a pained sigh. "The house," I admit. "It's that fucking house."

"The one you built?"

Without opening my eyes, I nod. "That's the one."

"But you showed me pictures of it. It's gorgeous!" she exclaims.

"Yeah, maybe if it wasn't sinking into the fucking swamp and overrun by ghosts."

There. I said it. Ghosts.

"Ghosts?" Ellie parrots. "Like, for real?"

"Maybe," I groan. "I don't know. It's just creepy. Even when I'm home alone, it always feels like there's somebody watching me. There are noises, things moving, that sort of stuff."

"Have you ever seen anything? Like an apparition or whatever?" Ellie asks eagerly.

I open one eye and glance at her. She really is quite sexy, in a generic sort of way. Her blonde hair is thick and tumbles over her shoulders in carefully styled waves. Her face is a plastic surgeon's playground, full of fillers and Botox. I doubt even her breasts are authentic, though I'm certainly not complaining.

There are a thousand things I could be doing with a woman like this, and talking about a haunted house isn't one of them.

Sensing that I've got other things on my mind, Ellie pouts those perfectly sculpted lips and begs, "Please? Just tell me one story, I'm dying to know!"

After a few seconds of indecision, punctuated by her staring enticingly up at me from beneath her lashes, I capitulate, "Fine. But only one." I think about all the incidents that have happened over the last six months since we've moved in, but finally, I decide to tell her about the builder.

"We hired a local construction crew to clear the debris from the lot and rebuild the house," I start. "The contractor was this guy, I think his name was Tyson? Tyler? Something like that. But anyway, all these weird things started happening at the construction site. All the batteries on the power tools would be drained overnight, locked doors would be open in the morning, stuff like that. We all thought that maybe some homeless guy was living out in the swamp and coming up at night to mess with everything."

"Well, was there?" Ellie inquires.

I shake my head. "I don't think so. There were some accidents too. Some guy fell out a window and nearly fucking died in our driveway. Can you imagine what a mess that would have been for our insurance? And then some poor asshole put a nail through his hand a few weeks later. Meanwhile, every time I'm in town to walk through the property, I start hearing that the place is cursed."

Ellie's eyes widen. "Seriously?"

"I mean, that's what they said. And then just when we're a week or two out from completion, the contractor, Trevor or whatever his fucking name is, goes crazy. He just snaps, starts doing weird shit around town and raving to people that there are demons in the swamp. Then one night, he just disappears."

"Just like that?" Ellie gasps.

"The foreman said he was there one day, gone the next. But it sounds like something horrible happened in the house the night the contractor went missing. The foreman told me that there was blood all over the place, especially in the kitchen."

"Oh my God!" I can tell the story is scaring her, and I hate to admit that I'm a little pleased by her reaction. "Do you think he's dead?"

"Who knows?" I shrug, conveniently leaving out another detail the foreman had shared, which was that he had ended up locating the contractor in Florida a few weeks later, apparently tending to a family emergency.

Ellie suppresses a shudder, and I wrap my arms around her comfortingly, drawing her into my chest. "I can see why you always want to get away from there," she whispers against my skin.

"It's horrible," I agree. "In fact, I'm inconsolable."

Recognizing the playfulness in my tone, Ellie draws back. "I'd better console you then," she says slyly as her hands slide down my chest and further south.

"I think you should," I say.

And then I lie back and let her.

3

DING DONG DITCH

JULIA

THE MORNING IS BLINDINGLY BRIGHT AND DAMP AS HELL.

"Shit!" I yelp as I jump up from the rocking chair I've just sat in. I should've realized that all of the furniture out here on the back porch would be soaking wet after last night's rain. The sun has only been up for a few hours, and with the humidity churning the air into a soupy mess, nothing has even begun to dry out from the thunderstorm.

I really fucking hate it out here. Even the house's redeeming qualities, like the luxurious deck, are rendered useless by the swamp and the unrelenting Louisiana weather.

"This is why we can't have nice things," I mutter grumpily as I raise my mug to my lips and take a sip. At least the coffee's good. Thank God for small mercies.

My original plan had been to settle out here with my morning coffee in an attempt to make peace with the swamp. Obviously, nature isn't too keen on this tentative truce, so I resign myself to leaning against the railing with the ceramic mug clasped between my

15

hands. The rising steam blurs the air, and I squint through it at the lush greenery of the surrounding landscape.

Beyond the lawn, the ground softens into churning brown mud punctuated by pools of festering brackish water. The trunks of ancient cypress trees protrude from the depths like the prehistoric bones of some forgotten creature. Sunlight filters through the dense canopy of leaves, painting the air beneath with a hazy greenish glow. Insects whir and chirrup in the scraggly underbrush while birds wail to one another between the branches.

The cemetery is partially hidden by greenery, but its presence is inescapable. Yesterday, the workmen had removed two more gravestones and tiny coffins before leaving, and I had done my best not to look. There are still a lot left out there, however, and I know that the crew will be back in about an hour to pull yet more bodies from their watery crypts. I've already decided that I don't want to be out here when they're working. Some things are better left up to the imagination.

At the stark reminder of death's proximity, I decide that I've had enough of the great outdoors for one day, and I retreat into the blissful chill of the air conditioned kitchen.

I only get a few minutes of peace before the doorbell rings, sending a harsh double chime echoing through the empty halls. Wincing at the unexpected noise, I leave my coffee on the kitchen island and bustle toward the front door. For a moment, I consider who might be visiting at such an early hour, but then I realize that it must be the workmen checking in before they get started for the day. After all, it's not like I have any friends here who'd be swinging by.

But when I pull the door open, there's nobody there.

"Hello?" I call, peering out into the sun-drenched morning.

Only the insects answer, humming wildly, unseen in the cypress trees.

Nothing moves. There are no trucks in the driveway, no indication that the workmen have arrived, or of anybody else for that matter. Cold dread settles in the pit of my stomach as I freeze on the threshold.

Somebody had rang the doorbell. I know I hadn't imagined it.

"It's the wiring," I whisper out loud, trying to convince myself. "It's like Jake said. It's a new house. Something weird just happened with the wiring."

I know that's not the truth, even if I can't explain it. But there isn't really anything I can do about it, is there? The only solution is to close the door, make sure it's locked, and try to forget about it.

So I ignore the frantic pounding of my heart and do just that, slamming the door shut and turning the latch until the deadbolt slides home with a satisfying click.

I start back toward the safety of the kitchen but only make it a few steps before a new sound slices through the quiet.

Creak.

Freezing instantly, my eyes crawl up toward the ceiling where the noise came from.

There are a few seconds of tense silence, and then a quick pattering noise overhead followed by a high, child-like giggle turns my blood to ice in my veins.

Footsteps.

A child's footsteps.

Without thinking, I fly to the stairs and barrel up them toward the second floor, determined to pinpoint the source of the noise.

But as soon as I burst onto the landing, the footsteps instantly cease, as though somebody had simply hit pause.

The hallway is empty.

"What the fuck?" I gasp.

Am I going crazy? Had I just imagined it?

The memory of the workmen loading those tiny coffins onto their trucks yesterday pops into the forefront of my mind. Maybe that's what triggered this, I realize. I'd found the sight so jarring, and now my lonely, pre-coffee brain is interpreting totally normal noises as ghost children running through the corridors. The thing with the phantom visitor right before probably didn't help, either.

But just when I think I have the whole thing rationalized, the familiar two notes of the doorbell filter up from the first floor.

Anger replaces the cold fear in my chest. Whether it's spirits, my tired mind, or somebody just playing a stupid prank on me, I'm sick of it. In fact, I'm fucking done.

I stomp back downstairs, fuming. By the time I reach the front door, I'm in an absolute rage. I fling the door open and growl, "This isn't fucking funny!"

To my utter shock, there's actually somebody there.

An older lady with graying hair takes a step back, her eyes widening in surprise and concern at my uncouth greeting. She looks familiar, and it takes me a beat to realize that this is our closest neighbor, Helen.

"Oh my God, I am so sorry," I babble, my face reddening with embarrassment as it sinks in that I've just yelled incoherently at an elderly woman. "I've had somebody ding-dong-ditching me all morning, and I just thought…. Well, I don't know what I thought. I'm so sorry!"

Helen, recovering quickly from the misunderstanding, waves her hand dismissively. "Don't you worry about it, honey. I just stopped over with some muffins," she explains, holding out a basket covered with a pretty yellow cloth.

"That's so kind of you," I say. Normally, I'd just take the muffins and not bother fostering any social connections in this dump, but my loneliness and the hot dread I'd felt earlier urge me to ask, "Would you like to come in for a cup of tea?"

The older woman hesitates. Her eyes dart up to the house, stopping on each of the windows as though she expects to see somebody there. Finally, she replies, "Yes, thank you. That would be lovely." But even as I hold the door open for her to step inside, I notice that the tension never quite leaves her shoulders.

"I don't think you've been inside, have you?" I inquire politely as I lead her into the kitchen.

"No, I haven't," Helen confirms. "I haven't even set foot on the property since Ms. Penny lived here. It was shortly before the fire, in fact. You've done a beautiful job, though. How do you like it here?"

"It's a nice house," I say carefully. "I'm still getting used to it."

We reach the kitchen, and I offer Helen a stool at the island. She settles onto it as I go through the process of filling the kettle and placing it on the stove. We make small talk as the water boils and the tea brews, chatting about the life I'd left back in New York and Helen's husband, who I have yet to meet.

"And what about your man? Is he at home?" Helen asks. It's a casual enough question, but there's something in her tone that makes me think that this is more than just simple curiosity.

"No," I reply slowly. "He's away on business."

"So he doesn't spend much time here?" she probes.

I shake my head. "Honestly, he's gone more often than he's not. So it's mainly just us girls. And by us, I mean me."

"You must be awfully lonely out here," she observes keenly. "I bet your imagination runs wild in a big house like this, especially once the sun sets."

A shiver slides down my spine as I once again have the uncanny feeling that Helen's words hold a double meaning. Deciding to test that theory, I inquire, "Have you heard the stories about this place? About the ghosts in the swamp?"

Helen's eyebrows shoot up at the directness of my question, and I realize that the elderly woman had, in fact, been fishing. "Everybody knows the legends," she says after a moment.

"And are they true?"

"In a way." Her eyes dart around the kitchen, as though she's worried somebody might be listening. "Has anything weird happened since you moved in? Anything that would make you feel unsafe?"

I shrug. "Normal house stuff. Pipes and creaky floorboards and some bad wiring. No ghosts though, sorry."

The older woman doesn't look convinced, and when she speaks again, earnestness sparks like flint in her eyes. "If things ever get too strange, my door is always open."

"Thank you," I reply, thinking that this conversation was already far too strange for my tastes. At the same time, I have to admit that I'm grateful for her company, which lasts until the crunch of gravel outside indicates that the work crew has arrived.

Helen and I exchange our goodbyes, and I escort her to her car, greeting the workmen on the way. Before she drives off, she rolls her window down and catches my eye. "Remember what I said, Julia. You can always call me if you need help."

And then she rolls away, waving brightly.

What an odd lady.

By the time her vehicle disappears around the cypress-lined bend, I'm already dripping with sweat. Did I mention I hate the humidity? All I want to do is take a cold shower and bask in the air conditioning.

I turn around to make my way back to the house and find myself face to face with a stranger. Surprised, I let out a yelp and stumble back. It only takes a moment for me to realize that the man must be part of the work crew, though I don't recall having seen him the day before.

Eyes the color of molten honey meet mine. Sunlight filters through his fine blond hair. It gives an illusion of a golden halo spreading around his head, which compliments the strong lines of his jaw. He looks like the kind of guy you'd find playing baseball in the Midwest, not out here in the middle of a swamp.

My gaze trails down to his chest. He's muscular, but it's clear that he's built his bulk through hard labor, not long hours at the gym and endless cans of protein powder. He's wearing a white, buttoned shirt with the sleeves rolled to his elbows and tan trousers held up with suspender. It's a good look, I decide. In fact, the whole package nearly leaves me speechless.

"I... I'm sorry," I stammer, apologizing for the second time that day. "I didn't realize you were right there!"

He smiles warmly. "The apology is all mine, ma'am. I'm sorry to have startled you."

"It's fine," I assure him. He seems sweet, even if he speaks a little formally, and I sure won't be forgetting those glowing honey eyes anytime soon.

"You have a fine morning, ma'am." He nods.

He turns and heads toward the swamp, leaving me standing in the driveway.

Melancholy overtakes me as I watch his retreating form. Maybe being haunted wouldn't be such a bad thing.

At least I wouldn't feel so alone.

I turn back toward the house and take a few steps, but then, I can't help myself. I want to see him again.

When I turn back around, he's gone.

Thinking he must've been walking faster than I realized, I go inside to take that cold shower.

4

THE ARTIFACT

Zeke

JULIA.

I overheard her introducing herself to the foreman yesterday, which is how I learned her name.

My mind conjures the memory of her staring up at me, lips slightly parted and eyes widened in surprise. I do feel bad for having startled her earlier. She'd seemed so shaken up. It makes me wonder if something else has happened to her today, something unexplainable.

From where I stand amidst the crumbling tombstones jutting out of the cemetery, I peer through the twisted trunks of the cypress trees toward the house. The white façade shines like ivory beneath the unrelenting summer sun. Neat rows of windows gleam, and my eyes roam upward as I catch a flash of movement in one of them.

Julia, wrapped in nothing but a towel, walks past. Her long auburn hair is twisted up in a bun, but a few strands have escaped to frame her face. She doesn't seem to realize that anybody could see her. My gaze lowers to the spot where the top of the towel conceals her chest before the guilt kicks in.

23

I immediately turn away, blushing furiously. That's no way to treat a lady. My own mother, God rest her soul, would have whooped me for doing such a thing. Besides, there are a thousand reasons why I shouldn't even let myself consider Julia in such a way, one of the biggest being that she's married.

My heart sinks further as the face of her husband, Jake, looms in my thoughts. The man is devilishly handsome and exudes a sort of rakish energy that I could never muster. Plus, he's clearly wealthy. How else could he afford to build a place like this? I've seen his extensive collection of sports, cars and it must be costing more than a small fortune to disinter all of these graves and drain the swamp.

No, even if the circumstances were different, there's no way I'd ever be able to compete with somebody like Jake Carter. After all, what could I possibly offer Julia that he couldn't provide?

And yet, the woman in question didn't seem to be happy.

Even though I'd done some laboring jobs on the property in the past, I'd only just returned yesterday due to the work in the graveyard, so it isn't like I've seen much of their relationship. But still, the tension between the couple had been palpable yesterday. Jake had looked like he couldn't wait to be gone. Hell, he hadn't even given his wife a proper kiss goodbye.

After Jake had left, Julia's loneliness had seemed so obvious. I'd analyzed her carefully as she bent over one of the freshly uprooted tombstones a few minutes after her husband pulled out of the driveway.

"Hezekiah James," she had read, sounding out the unfamiliar name with some confusion. And then she had shivered in spite of the cloying heat of the day before retreating back inside the gleaming, monstrous house.

She'd seemed even more spooked this morning. Did something happened in the house? Did she see something?

It wouldn't surprise me. I've spent my fair share of time out at the old Gregory place, and it would be a lie to say that I've never experienced anything out of the ordinary. I've heard strange noises, seen shadows shift out in the swamp.

And there are darker things out here, too, things buried beneath centuries of mud that are not so easily exhumed. There are graves, old and unmarked, that should be left untouched.

Some things were never meant to be unearthed.

It worries me that Julia's here. I've resided in Hahnville for quite some time now, and I know the stories as well as I know my own name. I've heard all of the theories about witches and demons, ghosts and curses. Frankly, I'm inclined to believe them.

What else could explain all of the people who have gone missing over the years? There have been murders, too. At one point, the police had been adamant that a serial killer was on the loose in town, though their investigations had dredged up nothing but whispers and superstition. Suicides run rampant, and it's well known that several women have gone insane on the property over the years.

I think back to Miss Penny, the previous owner of the property. She had almost met a similar fate not too long ago. Riddled with health problems and tended to by a team of nurses and doctors, she kept the old house from collapsing into the swamp through nothing but sheer willpower. That is, until a mysterious fire broke out and burned the building to the ground, nearly taking the old woman with it.

But Miss Penny escaped, along with the nurses and a lodger. Luckily, no lives were lost that day. And now, like a phoenix rising from the ashes, the new house built by the Carters stands partially on the old foundation, defiant against the ancient tangle of marsh that lays siege to its borders.

I hoped that this building, all shiny and new, would mark the start of a better era for the property. Perhaps new bones and new blood would be enough to break the cycle of horror that has played on repeat for centuries.

As I stare up at the house, my eyes dutifully sliding over the window in which Julia previously appeared, that hope feels like silt sliding through my fingers to sink into the depths of the swamp.

Something spooked Julia.

I'm sure of it. Even now, surrounded by workmen out in the

cemetery, I can feel hungry eyes staring through me. I wonder if the others notice too.

As if on cue, one of the men calls out, "Hey, I think I've found something!"

"What, your brain?" another asks as he straightens up and leans on the shovel.

"Very funny," the first guy scoffs, rolling his eyes. "It's a box, I think."

The foreman drops his shovel and ambles over to where the man stands, item in hand. It does indeed look like a metal box, though it's caked in years' worth of putrid mud and debris.

"Looks old," the foreman comments. "Maybe somebody buried a pet?"

I shake my head. I have a terrible feeling that whatever is in there is definitely not somebody's deceased poodle, but nobody seems to pay me any mind.

"Let's open it and find out."

Unease swirls through me at the suggestion. Every ounce of my soul screams that this is wrong, that we should just toss this thing back in the swamp where it belongs. But the rest of the men working here don't seem to notice anything's amiss. They look intrigued, captivated, as though the box itself is drawing them in.

Open it.

A voice slithers out from the swamp, wrapping around my brain and squeezing. It's cold and unnerving, like something imitating human speech but not quite getting it right.

Open it.

Let me out.

I clamp my hands over my ears. I can't tell if the voice is just in my mind or if the others can hear it too.

The foreman holds out his hands in a silent request for the box, and the worker offers it wordlessly. Both wear the same blank expression. Their eyes are bright, almost feverish, never once straying from the grimy object.

This is wrong. The surety of it surges through me as the foreman uses his fingers to pry the thick mud away from the latch and hinges. I want to speak, to reach out and knock the box from his hands, but I'm frozen.

"It's locked," the man snarls as he pushes the grime away to reveal an ancient padlock. Anger flashes in his eyes, and he slams the box down on the ground with enough force for it to sink a few inches into the mossy ground. The rest of us flinch at the outburst, and it's like a spell has been broken.

"Boss?" one guy asks tentatively. "You okay?"

There's no reply. Ignoring the worker completely, the foreman turns and snatches up his shovel, wrenching it from the earth where he had planted it only moments before.

"Boss?" the man repeats. This time, his voice is creased with fear as the foreman rounds on him, brandishing the shovel. "What are you doing?"

Eyes shimmering in the oppressive sunlight, the foreman stares emptily down as the box. His gaze is as blank as the windows of the house, blind and unseeing. He raises the shovel high in the air, and for one horrible moment, I think he's going to bring it down on the workman.

When he moves, he strikes like a snake. The shovel flashes as it descends before it connects with the metal box with a sickening crack.

"Holy fuck!" the original man shrieks, jumping backward out of range. "What the fuck are you doing?"

"We need to open it," the foreman says flatly.

"Yeah, well *I* need to not be decapitated by a fucking shovel," the guy spits back, crossing his arms in front of his chest.

The others chatter in agreement, but the foreman doesn't pay them any mind. Instead, he squats next to the box and pries the broken lock loose. Tossing the misshapen chunk of metal aside, he yanks the lid open and then freezes.

The putrid stench of death wafts toward me, and I have to fight back the urge to gag. Maybe there is a body, or part of one, buried in there after all.

"Oh God," one man heaves, grabbing the neck of his shirt and lifting it up over his mouth and nose. "What the hell is that smell?"

In spite of the rancid scent emanating from the box, I can't help but lean in to try to catch a glimpse of the contents. Different possibilities whirl through my mind as I strain to see the object inside clearly, each one more grisly than the last.

The foreman reaches into the box and holds the thing up to the sunlight.

"A rock?" a guy gasps. "That's it?"

That does seem to be it. It's a smooth river stone, unblemished and unremarkable. Though the box has clearly been lost to the mire for centuries, the rock itself is spotless.

But when he turns it over in his hands, a chill strikes me through the core of my being.

There are letters carved into the underside of the rock. They're sloppy and primitive, like the writing of a child. The text is a sharp contrast to the neatly chiseled, albeit mostly faded, letters on the surrounding tombstones. This scrawl is desperate and primal, a plea into the dark set in stone for centuries.

That, however, is not what haunts me now. No, it's what those letters spell that frightens me. It's a name I know well, one that's devoured my hope with pointed teeth and stalked me through my nightmares.

ASMODEUS.

Energy rushes through the clearing, whipping the cypress trees into a split-second frenzy. It fades before anybody else notices it, but I can feel him here now, more solid than he's ever been.

By opening that box, they broke the spell and freed him from his bindings. He'll be out for revenge now.

He'll be out for blood.

And with mounting horror, I realize who his first victim will be.

Julia.

He'll claim Julia as his own.

The shrill sound of music playing fills the air as the foreman leaps backward, the rock slipping from his hands. Everyone startles, backing up. The foreman says, "It's just my fucking phone," and reaches into his pocket, but he doesn't turn the music off right away. He puzzles over it for a moment, like he's never heard that song before.

Folks, I'm goin' down to St. James Infirmary, see my baby there...
She's stretched out on a long, white table, so sweet, so cold, so fair...

5

WELCOME HOME?

JAKE

The closer I get to the house, the worse I feel.

I notice it the moment I turn onto the winding drive that marks the entrance of the property. The car's tires slide on the muddy, rutted road, and the frame of the vehicle is so low that I swear I can feel my fillings rattle as I maneuver down the potholed path. For once in my life, I actually regret owning such a fancy ride. This wouldn't be happening in a truck or an SUV.

Cypress branches close in overhead, blotting out the sun with feathery leaves and twisted, mottled wood. The trunks churn on either side of me, grotesque in their stature. Thick underbrush creeps into the road. For a moment, it feels like I'm all alone in this wild place.

Dread mounts in my gut as I navigate the familiar turns of the drive. I have a terrible thought that the path will go on forever, that each twist in the road will simply guide me farther away from civilization.

But then the trees part, and the mud shifts to patchy gravel that crunches satisfyingly under my tires as I pull into the open expanse of the driveway, and I'm flooded with inexplicable relief.

I've made it.

As I glance up at the house, the one that was supposed to be our dream home, part of me wishes that I hadn't made it at all.

The building seems alive somehow. The windows, which had formerly shimmered blindly beneath the sun, now make me think of the glistening eyes of an arachnid, waiting with bated breath for an unwitting fool to step into its web. Ivy creeps up the sides of the previously spotless façade. There are patches of grime mottled across the siding, giving the house a moldy appearance.

How the hell has this place declined so fast? I've only been gone a week. But now, it looks like years have passed since I left. As much as I hate to admit it, it really does look like a haunted house.

"Fuck this," I mutter, shaking my head and turning the key in the ignition to kill the engine.

I'm barely out of the car before the front door swings open to reveal Julia. She looks perfect, as usual. Her auburn hair tumbles artfully over her shoulders. She's wearing a green dress that probably costs about as much as the sports car I've just exited. And, of course, she's got those ridiculous heels on, as if anybody would see her sporting them in this godforsaken place.

The ghost of an expression slides across her elegant features. It's not excitement, exactly. More like relief.

But from what?

"Hey, honey," I call as I drag my duffel bag and briefcase out of the passenger seat. "Miss me?"

"Of course," she replies dutifully. She leans in for a kiss, and I quickly grace her lips with a light peck. The memory of the blonde's plush mouth lingers in my mind as I pull away from my wife, guilt leaching into my veins.

I hate that I feel bad for my extracurricular activities. I shouldn't. I'm a man with needs, after all. And while Julia may turn heads at corporate parties and can charm the pants off of any C-suite occupant, sometimes I crave something a little warmer, more approachable. It's only natural.

"How was your trip?" Julia inquires as she takes the briefcase from my hand.

"Good," I assure her. "I've got the investors right where I want them. They'll all be signed on by the end of the week."

She shoots me a thin smile. "That's great news." I can practically hear the gears turning in her head, planning her next shopping trip using my hard earned money. I fight the urge to roll my eyes.

Instead, I say, "God, it's hot as hell here. I'm already sweating." Perspiration beads on my forehead and between my shoulder blades. The stench of the swamp permeates the humidity, clinging to my skin, hair, and clothes like poison. A strange electricity shudders, unseen, through the air, and I wonder if a thunderstorm is brewing.

"Go and take a shower," Julia urges as she ushers me through the front door and into the blissfully regulated temperatures of the air conditioned house. "I'll make dinner."

I know my wife means that loosely. I don't think she's ever properly cooked a day in her life. Instead, she's always ordered these meals where the ingredients come portioned out, and all she has to do is follow the directions. Honestly, I don't know why she even bothers. It's not like she does anything all day. Would it kill her to spend some time learning how to actually roast a chicken or fry an egg?

My sour mood only deepens as I shower. I can't seem to get the putrid smell of the marsh off me, no matter how hard I scrub. And I can't relax either, even with the state-of-the-art water jet shower head pounding down on my back. The skin on my neck is constantly prickling, as though somebody is watching me from the doorway of the bathroom. But every time I turn, there's nobody there.

God, I hate this fucking place.

When I finally sit down across from Julia at the vast dining room table, the only thing I want to do is eat in silence. Of course, she can't even do that one thing for me.

"I'm glad you're home," she starts as she spears a chunk of potato with her fork. "So many weird things have been happening, and it's been freaking me out." I don't want to hear it, but she continues anyway, "The doorbell rang on its own, and I heard what sounded like kids running around upstairs."

"Kids?" I scoff. "Don't be stupid."

"Seriously," she insists. "It started after they pulled up those coffins. I didn't realize how many children were buried out in the swamp. Just thinking about it gives me the creeps."

It makes my skin crawl too, but I'm not about to admit it and feed into her constant wailings about the house. "You and your active imagination," I dismiss. "You saw the coffins, and your brain just filled in the blanks. Honestly, Julia, you fit right in out here with all of the other superstitious freaks."

Her delicate features crease into a hurt frown. "I know what I heard," she snaps before falling silent.

The rest of dinner is blissfully quiet. She doesn't say a word to me as she clears the table. Once that's done, she sweeps past me, heading out into the hallway towards the stairs.

"Where are you going?" I call after her, trailing in her wake.

"Bed," she says in a clipped tone before disappearing up the stairs. I go to follow her but only make it halfway down the hallway before I realize that it's way darker than it should be. Peering up towards the ceiling, I notice that the bulb right inside the front door is dead, swathing the bottom of the steps in gloomy shadow.

Changing a bulb out is the last thing I feel like doing right now, but I know that if I ignore it, Julia will just nag me mercilessly about it later. Huffing, I trudge to the kitchen and, after digging through several cabinets, I find a box of light bulbs stuffed way in the back of one. I haul a stool away from the island on my way back out. Otherwise I'd have to pick my way through the darkness to the garage and back to get the stepladder. I'd take my wife's wrath over that any day.

The process, though annoying, is quick and easy. Within minutes, I've finished my task and returned the stool to the kitchen. From there, I make my way upstairs to find Julia.

When I step into the master bedroom, I'm reminded of exactly why I married her in the first place.

She's in the process of changing into her nightgown. The green dress she'd been wearing lay discarded over the back of the vanity chair. My blood rushes south as I realize that she hadn't been wearing a bra underneath that expensive item of clothing. Now she's left in only an emerald green thong, those heels, and nothing else.

I move quickly, encircling her from behind with my arms as I nuzzle my nose into her perfect hair. Her lithe body tenses against mine. "I'm not in the mood," she sighs.

"Baby, I'm sorry," I cajole. How many times have we gone through this song and dance? "I shouldn't have been so mean to you. I'm sorry."

Julia doesn't say anything, but her muscles soften in my grasp as she melts at the apology. I take a risk and lift her hair away from her neck before kissing the soft skin there, and the little sigh she releases tells me I've won this battle.

She turns in my arms and presses her lips to mind, coaxing a proper kiss out of me. I'm very aware of her bare breasts pressing against my chest, and I don't bother to fight the urge to bring one hand up to caress the soft peak of her nipple.

A moan rolls from her lips, I decide I really can't wait any longer. I break away from her long enough to pull my shirt over my head and step out of my jeans before I push her back toward the bed.

She's gorgeous, splayed there on the duvet with only a thin strip of green fabric covering her cunt. Without pausing, I kick off my boxers, freeing my cock. Julia eyes it hungrily, pupils blown.

"Did you miss me?" I demand as I lower myself down so that I'm covering her slim form.

She bites her lip and nods.

That's all I need to hear.

I skim one hand down to the junction of her thighs, pushing the thong to one side to allow my fingers to brush her slick heat. I slide one digit inside as she gasps beneath me. God, she's so wet. Has she been sitting here the whole time I was gone, just waiting for me to come home and fuck her?

Well, I've never been one to keep a lady waiting.

I line my cock up with her entrance, hissing at the feel of her against my sensitive skin as I sink into her, inch by inch. Just when I'm fully sheathed inside of her, I pull out, leaving her whimpering for more. She doesn't have time to beg for me to fuck her before I thrust back in.

My hips move with measured strokes as her inner walls massage my cock. Soft, breathy noises spill from Julia's lips as she writhes beneath me. It doesn't take long for my pleasure to crest.

"Fuck," I groan as I thrust hard into her one last time. The release shudders through me as I spill myself into her pussy.

Panting, I roll off of her and collapse onto the mattress beside her. We lie there silently for a moment before I ask, "Was that good for you, baby?"

Julia fixes me with an unreadable stare. Her pupils are blown from lust, and her chest is heaving. "Yeah," she says after a moment before getting up and moving toward the bathroom.

Later, when she's back in bed, and I'm certain she's asleep, I watch her. My mind wanders back to the first night we spent in the house. That was the best sex we'd ever had. I don't know what came over us. It was like there was an animal inside of me, clawing at me to release it, and Julia met that energy deliciously. Where was that dynamic now?

The thought leaves me feeling strangely inadequate. There's no way I'm going to sleep now with my mind racing.

I get up and pull on my boxers before padding over to the window. I squint out into the swirling darkness, surveying the swamp. It looks far more sinister a night, I decide. It takes a few seconds for my eyes to adjust enough to pick out the individual tree trunks rising out of the mire. Finally, my gaze fixes on the raised mound of the cemetery. I can just make out the eldritch edges of the tombstones there, as well as the bare patch of ground where several of the graves have already been removed.

I can't wait until that monstrosity is gone and the marsh is drained for good. I've already got plans for a tennis court and a pool once the job is done.

I'm about to turn away from the window when I notice a flash of something darting between the decrepit headstones. I press my face closer to the window, straining to make sense of what I'm seeing.

There's a man in the swamp.

Not just any man, I realize. Isn't that the builder, the guy who went crazy and disappeared? His name was Tyler or something.

But he looks wrong, somehow. I can't put my finger on it, exactly, but there's something about the way he's moving that isn't natural. It's like watching a four legged animal run on its hind legs.

"What the fuck?" I mutter.

As if he heard me, the man freezes and raises his head. I can't explain how, but I swear that his eyes are fixed on mine. Every nerve in my body screams out in warning, and my stomach churns in sudden terror.

I've never been one to run toward danger, and I'm not about to start now. There's no way in hell I'm going out there to check it out. Instead, I raise a shaking hand and pull the blinds closed. Then I dart out of the room and down the stairs to check that the front door is locked.

When I'm satisfied the house is secure, I lean back against the door and sigh in relief. Now that I think about it, what would that guy possibly be doing in the swamp so late at night? It's so dark out, my eyes probably played tricks on me. Isn't that what I keep telling Julia?

"There's nothing out there," I whisper. Even so, I reach for the light switch and turn it on. I don't want to stand in the shadows any longer.

Light spills from the bulb, and I sigh again. But seconds later, the light flickers, and then the bulb breaks with a sharp crack.

I'm plunged into darkness.

"There's nothing out there," I mutter again.

But now, I'm not so sure.

6

SOMEONE'S IN THE HOUSE

I'M NOT SURE WHAT WAKES ME.

It's not the sun, that's for sure. For some reason, the blinds are firmly shut, blocking the early morning light from filtering in through the glass.

I blink the sleep from my eyes as I peer into the surrounding dimness. I'm lying in bed, the covers tangled around my legs as though I'd thrashed in my slumber. A dull soreness at the juncture of my thighs reminds me of exactly what Jake and I had been doing last night.

But where is Jake now?

His side of the bed is empty, the sheets cold and untouched.

"Jake?" I call. My voice sounds muted in the still morning air.

There's no response.

Sighing, I extract myself from the blankets. Goosebumps rise on my arms as the cool, conditioned air kisses my skin. I grab my robe and shrug it on against the chill before padding over to the bathroom.

Like the bedroom, there's no sign of Jake. I frown. This isn't like him. Sure, he's usually an early riser, but he's not exactly quiet in the mornings. He runs the shower at full blasts, bustles around in the bathroom, and stomps down the stairs without a care in the world. But I haven't heard a peep from him today, and that worries me more than I care to admit.

Maybe he's in his office, I consider. That's where he spends most of his time when he's home. I'm not convinced that he actually does a lot of work in there, but he has been making a habit of disappearing off into the room and brooding for a couple of hours.

Still, something doesn't feel right. I'm keenly aware of the sour thread of unease coiling in the pit of my stomach as I move quietly out into the hallway. The hardwood floor is cold beneath my bare feet. Every step I take seems far too loud and by the time I reach the stairs, I feel like a scared little kid again, creeping my way through a haunted house and hoping that the monsters don't hear me.

"Get a grip," I mutter to myself. I really am being ridiculous. Whether there are ghosts here or not, this is my home. There's no reason to sneak around like some intruder. I force myself to stand up a little straighter as I intentionally stomp down the stairs. Dread wells in my throat with each step, but I swallow it down.

This is just a normal morning, I tell myself. Jake is probably just working in his office. I'll go to the kitchen and make us some coffee. I'm sure he'll appreciate a fresh cup after getting up so early.

But even with these thoughts running through my mind, I can't seem to shake the anxiety I'd felt earlier. I almost sigh with relief as I make it to the bottom of the stairs and turn toward the kitchen.

A glint of glass on the floor prompts me to stop in my tracks. It's lucky that I noticed it, I realize. My bare toes are only inches from the shards, and I hate to think of what would have happened if I hadn't seen them.

Confusion rolls through me as I bend down to inspect the fragments. After a moment of studying the curved slivers and the silvery metal pieces strewn between them, I realize that they must be the remnants of a light bulb.

"Weird," I murmur as I straighten and glance up at the light fixture. The bulb went out the day before. I'd hoped that Jake would've noticed and fixed it, but I should have known better than to think he'd actually do something useful around the house. It must have popped somehow.

Stepping carefully around the glass, I continue on my way to the kitchen. I put the coffee on and then grab the dustpan. By the time I clean up the glass in the hallway, the espresso machine is letting out its last few gurgles. The rich smell of the caffeinated beverage curls through the air, and for the first time that morning, I let myself relax a bit.

Once the coffee is ready, I pour out two mugs, adding cream and sugar to one and leaving the other black, the way Jake likes it. I'm just gathering both up when I hear footsteps on the stairs heading down from the second floor landing.

I suddenly feel a bit silly. Jake must have been somewhere upstairs this whole time. The realization is reinforced as I hear him move through the ground floor toward his office. Seconds later, the door slams.

He must have gotten an urgent work call or something. Maybe he'd been up all night dealing with an emergency or a difficult client. In that case, I'm sure he won't mind me interrupting if it means a solid dose of caffeine.

I trail after him, weaving through the rooms until I come to the closed door of his office. As I approach, I can see the shadow of his form spilling out from the gap in the threshold. He looks like he's pacing back and forth. Whatever he's dealing with, it seems stressful.

Unable to knock with my hands full, I say, "Jake? Want some coffee?"

He stops moving, but he doesn't answer. The door remains closed.

"Jake?" I ask again.

The knob turns, and the door creaks inward about an inch. "Wow, thanks for the help," I quip, rolling my eyes as I push into the room.

There's nobody there.

"What the fuck?" I gasp. My eyes roam the corners of the vacant space, but there isn't exactly anywhere for somebody to hide. The walls are lined with bookshelves and filing cabinets, and the only other furniture is Jake's massive desk. The chair sits empty. The monitors are all blank and powered down. There's no sign anybody had been here at all.

But I know what I heard.

I know what I saw.

Fear claws at my nerves as I back quickly from the room. Moving as fast as I can without spilling the coffee, I hurry back to the kitchen. I'd left my phone charging there overnight, and I find it now on the island, right where it should be.

My first instinct is to call Jake, but when I take a look at my notifications, I realize there's no point.

A text from my husband is waiting for me on the screen.

Sorry honey. A work thing came up, and I had to leave for NOLA. I'll be back in a few days. I promise I'll make it up to you.

According to the timestamp, he'd sent the message around 2:00 in the morning.

So if it wasn't Jake in the office, who was it?

"Fuck this," I proclaim to the kitchen. I slide my phone into the pocket of my robe, gather up both mugs of coffee, and speed walk toward the front door. I don't know why, but my nerves are screaming that I need to get out of here. I have the worst feeling that there's something following me, something at my back and hot breath on my neck.

Turn around, Julia.

The voice is like the gurgle of mud in the swamp, inhuman, something not meant to be heard. I can't tell if it's in my head or out loud, but there is no fucking way I'm going to do as it asks.

I reach the front door and burst out into the sticky heat. In my cloud of panic, I barely notice the workman standing there until I nearly crash into him.

"Oh God, I'm sorry!" I exclaim. Coffee sloshes out of the mugs I'm holding and splashes down onto the gravel, luckily missing both of us. Flustered, I glance up at the man and blush as I realize that it's the guy I ran into the other day.

"Ma'am, are you okay?" he asks, concern creasing through his eyes. I'm struck again by how handsome he is, which only deepens my embarrassment.

"Yeah, I'm fine," I manage. "I... I'm sorry. I'm kind of making a habit of this, I guess."

The man nods kindly. We stand there awkwardly for a moment, him watching me carefully with honey colored eyes as I linger with a half-spilled mug of coffee in each hand.

"Want some help?" he asks eventually, gesturing to the mugs.

I consider him for a second. There's absolutely no way I'm going back in the house right now, and I'd rather not be alone. Would it really be so wrong of me to ask him to keep me company? After all, Jake's basically abandoned me. Why should I feel bad?

Making up my mind, I hold one of the mugs out to him. "Actually, would you like some coffee? I made some for my husband, but he had to go out. It'd be a shame to waste it."

The man regards the cup warily. A fearful expression flits across his face, which strikes me as odd. What's so scary about a cup of coffee? But then he reaches out and closes his fingers around the offered mug, lifting it easily out of my grasp. Relief replaces the nervousness in his eyes, only adding to my confusion.

He flashes me a broad, warm smile, and all of my concern melts away. "Thank you, ma'am," he grins. "That's awfully kind of you."

"Oh, please don't call me ma'am," I insist. "Julia is just fine."

"It's a pleasure to make your acquaintance," he replies, his voice a cozy rumble. "I'm Zeke."

I can't help but smile at the formality of his speech. Maybe this place really does have some old world charm after all. "You're here early, Zeke. I don't think the rest of the crew is here yet. Are you really that excited about wading through the swamp?"

He lets out a deep chuckle. "Not exactly. I'm local, but the rest of the guys come from pretty far out of town. You know, because of all the spooky stories. Nobody closer wanted to take the job."

"So you're from Hahnville?" I ask, intrigued. Truthfully, I haven't made much of an effort to get to know anybody here, aside from

Helen. If all of the guys in town are this cute, maybe I've been seriously missing out.

Zeke nods. "I've been here for a long time."

"So you must know all about the history of this place?"

"More than most," he confirms. His honeyed eyes flit out toward the swamp and then back to mine.

I take a tentative sip of my coffee before I pose my next questions. "Do you think the swamp is haunted?"

"I think there's a lot about this place that people weren't meant to ever know," he replies carefully. "Why do you ask?"

For a moment, I want to tell him everything, about the footsteps and the voice and the feeling of always being watched. But it's crazy. He'll just say the same thing as Jake, that it's all in my head. It's a big house in a strange place. My mind is bound to play tricks on me, especially when I've been spending so much time out here alone.

And so I shrug, "Just curious."

Zeke's eyes narrow skeptically, but he doesn't have a chance to say anything before the sound of tires on gravel crunches through the still morning. A few seconds later, the work crew's trucks roll into view.

"I guess it's time to go," Zeke sighs. He presses the mug back into my hand. "Thanks for the coffee, Julia. It was nice talking to you."

"Likewise," I assure him, matching his warm smile with one of my own. I glance over my shoulder back at the house. I really don't want to go back in. Maybe I should ask Zeke to come in and look around in case somebody really had broken in last night. An intruder is, after all, far more likely than an infestation of ghosts.

But when I turn back around, Zeke is already gone.

I shiver in spite of the growing warmth of the day. He must have gone around the side of the house, but he moved so quickly and quietly. I shake my head. Zeke's been nothing but polite and sweet. He has the sort of old world charm that Jake would never be able to muster.

But he's gone off to do his work, which is why he's here in the first place. And I'm not going to let this house get the better of me. It's broad daylight, for heaven's sake. I'm stupid for being afraid to go back inside.

I reluctantly make my way toward the front door after offering the workmen a wave. Even though I know it's ridiculous to be scared of my own home, I still don't want to be entirely alone, so I pull out my cell phone, and clutching the handles of both empty mugs in one hand, dial my best friend Nina.

She picks up immediately with a cheerful, "Hey, girl!"

"Hey," I greet her back as I step inside of the house.

"Is everything okay? It's kind of early for you," Nina says.

"Yeah," I lie. "It's just that Jake's gone on another business trip, and I'm just kind of freaking myself out."

I can practically hear Nina's eyes roll over the phone. "Another one? Seriously, Julia, it's time to consider that maybe Jake isn't being totally honest with you."

It's not something I want to think about right now. Instead, I tell her, "It's not like that. I'm only calling because this house gives me the fucking creeps. I scared myself so bad this morning that I went out and had coffee with one of the workmen."

"Ooh!" Nina gasps. "Is he cute?"

It's my turn to roll my eyes. "For the record, yes. But why does that even matter?"

"Well, if Jake's off *working*, then why can't you do a little *work* too?"

"It was just a cup of coffee," I groan, shaking my head even though my friend can't see it.

"Honestly, Jules, would it really be so wrong of you to explore it?"

"I'm married," I shoot back.

"And so is Jake, but he doesn't seem to act like it," she retorts.

I close my eyes. As much as I hate to think about it, Nina's right. He doesn't. He leaves me here on my own and meanwhile, I have no idea what he's up to.

But he couldn't be cheating on me.

Could he?

I don't want to face the answer, but sooner or later, I know I won't have a choice.

7

HELP FROM BEYOND THE GRAVE

Zeke

God, I feel so *alive*.

I close my eyes and let the relentless eye of the sun beat down on me. What does it see when it looks at me? A man? Something more? Something less?

And what does Julia see, I wonder?

I know it's dangerous to let my thoughts wander down this path, but it's as though my mind has become untethered with possibilities. My hand curls around a phantom mug, remembering the feeling of the smooth porcelain against my palm and the heat radiating through my hand as Julia had questioned me with increasing interest.

I'd just had coffee with Julia Carter.

She wore no makeup, and her hair was mussed from sleep, but that had somehow only made her more beautiful. Her eyes, as green as moss, shone in the fresh morning light. I had the overwhelming urge to reach out and touch her, to brush my fingertips over the soft curve of her lips, but propriety stopped me in my tracks.

47

I wouldn't disrespect Julia like that. She is too good for me to be thinking about her in such a way.

To distract myself from my tumultuous thoughts, I instead consider why she had burst out of the house in a panic.

The answer is one I do not want to fathom.

Sighing, I turn and stare up at the house's looming façade. The building looks older somehow, like it's fraying around the edges. The siding is riddled with blooms of mottled mold and sagging in some places. The back porch seems crooked, as though one side of it has sunken slightly into the muddy ground. Tangles of ivy and brambles creep up the walls to peek into the windows, which glare out at the swamp in glassy stillness. I get the sense that the structure is watching me back, a predator surveying its prey.

But deep down, I know that I'm not the one it wants.

As if confirming my concerns, a low melody floats on the wind, stirring sour fear in my soul.

Folks, I'm goin' down to St. James Infirmary…

I move slowly to face the marsh, my eyes picking through the trunks of cypress trees and gnarled swathes of underbrush to locate the source of the haunting tune.

At first, I don't see anybody but the workers. They're levering a gravestone out of the loamy ground, sweating from the effort. None of them seem to hear what I do.

See my baby there, she's stretched out on a long, white table…

I can feel it in the air that something terrible is about to happen. I want to call out to the work crew in the swamp, but when I open my mouth, my voice gets stuck in my throat.

Panic wells in my chest. Don't they sense it? Don't they know that they're in danger?

So sweet, so cold, so fair…

The heavy tombstone the workers are gathered around slides in the mud, toppling down toward one of the crew. Shouts of alarm punctuate the air, followed by a wet thud, and then silence.

I don't want to look. I don't want to see how badly the gravestone has injured the man.

But then a shaky laugh filters through the trees, and I can't help but glance over.

To my immense relief, the worker is okay. He's sprawled out on the mossy ground, dangerously close to the hunk of granite lying beside him. He must have rolled out of the way at the last second, I realize.

"Holy shit!" the foreman exclaims, his voice audible on the still air. "You okay?"

The guy nods, though I can't quite hear his response. His face, however, tells the whole story. Relief, fear, confusion. It's clear he understands how close a call he just had, if not what caused it. I'll be surprised if he turns up for work tomorrow, or even if he finishes out the rest of today.

Satisfied that the man is as safe as anybody could be in a place like this, I double down on my efforts of scouring the swamp. I know the thing I'm looking for is here somewhere, lurking just out of sight.

A shadow flashes through the trees. For a moment, it appears to be as formless as smoke, but then the light shifts through the feathery leaves of the cypress branches to illuminate the solid edges of a man.

Several seconds pass, and we simply stare at one another.

It looks different from the last time I saw it, but it's unmistakable. There's something about the crooked posture and the tilt of its head that reminds me of a marionette on a string, as though I'm not so much looking at the thing itself but what it wants me to see.

Dread claws down my spine as I stand, transfixed, under its gaze. I'd hoped that the bastard wouldn't be back this time, that it had gone for good. But ever since the workmen pulled that artifact up from the mud, I'd known that this was inevitable. He was prowling around before. Now, he's fully energized.

It's no wonder Julia fled the house this morning, that she was so spooked.

"I won't let you have her," I snarl. Even as far away as it is, I know the figure in the swamp can hear me.

In response, a grin spreads over its face. Its lips draw back over its teeth as though the skin is made of wax, moving into a horrible parody of a smile. It raises one hand and waves. And then, as though it had never been there at all, it disappears into the shadows of the mire.

I glare out at the space it occupied. I can't just stand by and let this thing run free, not with Julia here in the house. But I can't do this on my own.

I'm going to need some help.

I turn back toward the home. There's an old woman standing on the porch, though her sudden presence doesn't startle me. She's a part of this land, just like the others. But unlike the thing out there in the swamp, she's not here to do harm.

The frail woman's eyes land on mine, and she smiles sadly at me. When she speaks, her voice is like the breeze through the cypress leaves and the patter of rain on a summer's evening.

"He's back, isn't he?" she asks.

"Yes, ma'am," I reply solemnly.

"Are you fixing to take care of him?"

I nod. "Somebody's got to."

"Good," she says. "About damn time."

As I watch, the woman's outline starts to fade until her form is indiscernible. I can still feel her there, though.

"Don't you worry, Miss Penny," I murmur into the empty morning air. "I'll take care of him, once and for all."

About damn time, indeed.

8

SOMETHING'S IN THE SHADOWS

Jake

I'M NOT A COWARD.

It's not like I was scared and ran away because a fucking light bulb broke, or because the ensuing darkness seemed bigger somehow, alive. No, it was because I simply had business to attend to. At least, that's what I tell myself as I pull up in front of the house at the edge of the swamp.

Julia probably hadn't even cared that I'd gone. After all, I'd texted her that I had to go out, and she hadn't ever responded. Did she even notice I left? God, she sure knows how to make a guy feel wanted in his marriage.

A streak of lightning skitters across the leaden sky, followed quickly by a peal of thunder so loud that the car practically rattles around me. It's not raining yet, though the clouds that loom overhead are the color of a fresh bruise and promise an imminent downpour. Not wanting to ruin my vehicle, I decide to park in the garage instead of the driveway.

The rain starts just as I pull inside. Water roars against the roof, and once closed, the automatic door does little to quell the sound. Couldn't the storm have held off for five more minutes so that I wouldn't have to run through the downpour over to the house from the detached garage?

No, that'd be far too much to ask. It's not like I've been on a lucky streak lately.

I think sourly about how this morning's business meeting had gone. One of the key investors dragged his feet, and now the whole operation is behind schedule. I've spent the whole day scrambling for a solution, except for the time it took to visit my favorite blonde, Ellie, in the city.

As if on cue, my phone buzzes to announce an incoming call. I wait for it to ring three times and then swipe to answer.

"Hello?" I ask.

"Howdy, Jake," Thurman greets in his usual manner. His voice is thready, barely audible over the static on the line and the echoed pounding of the storm beating down on the roof of the garage.

"Please tell me you've got good news," I sigh, pinching the bridge of my nose between my thumb and forefinger.

"Well, it certainly ain't bad," the man replies. "I couldn't get the investor to change his mind, but I was able to find some *product* that will get us through just fine. Our drivers will have them over the border by the end of the week."

"And you're sure there'll be no trouble if they get stopped?"

"I'm sure," Thurman confirms. "These guys do this all the time. They've got some sort of arrangement, if you catch my drift."

I nod. "Oh, I catch it all right. I just don't want anybody catching *me*."

Thurman lets out a sardonic chuckle. "Us, you mean. My ass is on the line too, boss. But don't you worry. There won't be any problems."

"There better not be," I warn. "Anything else?"

"Nope."

"In that case, let me know when they get here. As soon as those workers arrive, I want them set up and ready to hit the job site. Got it?"

"Sure thing. Good night, boss," Thurman says before hanging up.

I slide my phone into my pocket and slump back against the car. Unease squirms in my gut. I know that what we're doing is, perhaps, technically a bit beyond the confines of legality. But if I don't have workers for my construction company, then the other investors will pull out and kill the venture before it even has a chance to start. This is my only option. In spite of how hard we've worked to cover our tracks, I'm still dreading what might happen if we get caught.

I'd probably get tossed in jail. My business would go under, and I'd be fined into oblivion. What would Julia think? Would she care about what happened to me, or would she just be concerned about how she will fund her next shopping trip?

I can't let myself go down this route. Chances are, everything will go smoothly, and my new company will boom. The risks will be worth it.

Mustering up my energy, I straighten up and walk toward the garage door. I'm only a few steps away from the button that controls it when I hear a thud on the roof at the far end of the building.

I freeze. Maybe it was a branch? A really heavy branch?

But then the thumping noise comes again, and again, and again, moving rhythmically in a straight line toward where I'm trembling beside the door.

Footsteps.

It sounds like footsteps.

There's no way they belong to an animal. They're too heavy, and the stride is too long. It sounds like a man strolling around up there, but that would be ridiculous.

Anxiety prickles along the back of my neck as the footsteps stop directly above me. I strain to pick up any movement, but the rain is so loud, and the blood thundering through my veins is suddenly deafening that I can't hear anything at all.

And then the car revs to life, and I nearly jump out of my skin.

Even though I can feel the cold outline of the key in my pocket, the car is on. The headlights shine against the far wall as the engine purrs, and the radio flicks through the stations before settling on one.

A few measures of a slow, haunting tune filter out into the enclosed space, fighting to be heard above the storm.

Terror rises in my throat as I jolt into motion. Lunging forward, I slam the button for the garage door. The door rumbles and begins to open. It seems to take an eternity, and the whole time that song is blaring.

As soon as the door opens a few feet, I drop down and scuttle underneath. Mud squelches beneath my palms and smears onto my pants as I fall onto the soupy driveway. It's only when I've staggered back to my feet that I turn back to the garage.

The door finishes opening, revealing a dark and silent interior. The noise of the motor is gone. The radio is silent. The car is off.

"What the fuck?" I choke out, barely noticing as the rain pummels down onto my clammy skin.

The garage door stutters to life again and starts to close. I stand and watch until it's entirely shut. I'm rooted in place by the strength of my fear.

And then the spell is broken, and I'm suddenly very aware of the rain running down my skin in lukewarm torrents and soaking through my clothes. I back away from the garage, half-expecting the door to open again, but it doesn't.

"Jake?"

I startle at the familiar voice sounding from the house behind me.

"Jake? What the hell are you doing standing out in the rain like that?" Julia calls. Reluctant to turn my back on the garage, I spin slowly to face my wife. She's standing in the doorway, looking as impeccable as ever with her arms crossed and a stern expression locked on her delicate features.

"Nothing," I grumble. I slog toward the threshold, though I can't help but glance back over my shoulder several times before I reach the front door.

Julia's frown doesn't lift as she steps back to let me pass. I kick my muddy shoes off almost immediately. They're probably ruined anyway.

"Where were you, Jake?" she asks. There's an edge to her tone that makes me uncomfortable, like she knows exactly where I've been. But how could she? I'm careful to never leave evidence of my affairs lying around. Maybe it's that stupid friend of hers putting ideas in her head. Or maybe Julia is just being her usual neurotic self.

"New Orleans, like I said in my text," I snap, irritated by her constant need to question my activities. So what if I am getting a bit on the side? She should trust what I say, not give me a hard time.

"Doing what, exactly?" she pushes.

Anger boils up inside of me, but I push it back. If I yell at her, she'll just take that as confirmation of whatever suspicions she's cooked up. Instead, I don't answer and brush past her up the stairs.

Once I'm in the master bedroom, I strip off my dripping, muddy clothes and dump them on the bathroom floor before jumping in the shower. I wash the muck off my body quickly and then wrap a towel around my waist.

When I walk out into the main room, Julia is waiting for me. She's perched on the edge of the bed, legs neatly crossed at the ankle.

I ignore her as I pull on a pair of sweatpants and a T-shirt, but the frosty silence doesn't last long.

"Where were you?" Julia repeats. Her voice is hard.

Squirming like an insect caught under a microscope, I say through gritted teeth, "I already told you."

"New Orleans is a big place, Jake. Were you at the office?" she needles. "Or somewhere else?"

"The office," I lie.

"The whole time?"

"The whole time."

"So why is it that when I called the office, they said you weren't there?"

The blood rushes out of my face as the implications of her words strike me. I stare at Julia, wide-eyed.

I'd always thought that she'd cry if she ever figured out what I'd been up to. She did last time, after all. I'd expected her to beg me for some other explanation, for some excuse to ease her pain.

But now she just watches me with those hard, gemstone eyes. Her pale face is set into a mask of disgust, as though I'm nothing more than dirt under one of her designer heels.

When she speaks, her tone is like ice. "I'd ask you where you really were, but we both know you'd only lie to me." She tosses me my phone from where I'd left it on the bed before my shower, and I catch it in numb hands. "You're sleeping in the guest room tonight."

And with that, she gets up, brushes some imaginary dust off the skirt of her dress, and strides out of the room.

It takes me a moment for the reality of the situation to sink in, and then the anger overtakes me.

Who the fuck does she think she is? Where would she be without me? I've given her everything: money, a beautiful house, everything she could ever fucking want. She should be kissing the fucking ground beneath my feet that I even looked at her twice, let alone married her.

Ungrateful bitch.

The thought stops me in my tracks. It's like a cold finger running across my brain, carving an icy path through my mind. I have the horrible feeling that it doesn't belong to me.

But it's true, isn't it? She *is* an ungrateful bitch.

I storm out into the hallway and up the stairs to the third floor. Those terrible thoughts whir through my brain as I burst into the guest room farthest from the landing and slam the door behind me.

The rage is overwhelming, threatening to consume me. I need to let off some steam, and what better way to do it than to stick it to Julia?

I unlock my phone and dial a familiar number. The line rings a few times before a sultry voice answers, saying, "Jake? Is that you baby?"

"Ellie," I sigh into the phone. I've already got one hand down the front of my sweatpants. My cock hardens in anticipation of what's to come.

"Is everything okay, sugar?" she asks in that sweet voice.

"Well, I've got a little problem," I drawl.

"Little? I wouldn't call it that," she teases. "Are you feeling lonely?"

"I could never be lonely with you around," I reply smoothly.

"I wish you were here," she confesses.

"And what would you do if I was?"

My fingers close around my cock as she tells me, in exquisite detail, what she'd do to me. I pump my length into my hand and imagine her mouth closing over my skin, of the feeling of the head of my shaft brushing against the back of her throat. I let my imagination run wild as she purrs down the line. Pleasure builds quickly and soon, I'm ready to come undone.

I let out a groan as I reach my release. Part of me hopes that Julia heard how some other woman made me come with only her voice.

It would serve her fucking right.

I've got no need for Ellie now that I've gotten what I needed, so I wrap the call up with her quickly. I use some tissues from the bedside table to clean up, turn off the lights, and then crawl into bed, exhausted.

It's strange, falling asleep alone in an unfamiliar room. The mattress is uncomfortable, and the sheets are new and scratchy. The light that filters in through the window seems different somehow, too. It also doesn't help that I'm on the top floor and the rain is loudest here.

My eyelids droop as the events of the day catch up with me. Just as I'm about to drift off to sleep, I catch a glimpse of a shadow in the corner, one that hadn't been there a second before.

I stare at it until sleep overtakes me, and in the second before I tumble into oblivion, I realize that the shadow has a face.

And I could swear that it's grinning.

9

A SLAP IN THE FACE

Julia

Tears well in my eyes, threatening to spill over. But I know that if I start crying, I won't be able to stop.

"Get a fucking grip," I mutter to myself.

I'm lying on the couch in the living room, attempting to watch my favorite reality TV show. After I confronted Jake earlier, I haven't been able to focus. Racing thoughts flutter through my brain like paper in the wind. I'd optimistically heated up a frozen dinner, but I'd only been able to pick at it before my nausea had overpowered my desire to eat. Now the meal sits, cold and congealed, on the coffee table, all but forgotten.

I know I could call Nina for support, but I don't want to go there until I have all of the facts. And the truth is, I don't really have many of those at all right now.

Yes, Jake's reaction to my questions all but confirmed my suspicions that he's nothing more than a cheating bastard. I have no doubt that he's up to his old tricks, but this time, I'm not going to let him off so easily. I need cold, hard proof.

59

And I know just how to get it.

I wait one hour–and then an extra few minutes for good measure. Once I'm sure that Jake must be asleep, I switch the television off. I don't want to be heard on my covert mission, so I take a moment to slip out of my heels and leave them placed neatly beside the couch.

It feels wrong, the thing I'm about to do, but I try not to dwell on it as I pad up the two flights of stairs until I reach the third floor. I heard Jake stomping around up here earlier. After noticing that only one door in the entire hallway is closed, it's easy to figure out which room he's chosen for the night.

Not wanting to wake him, I creep down the corridor until I reach the occupied guest room. I lean my ear against the door, listening for any sign that he might still be awake. When I hear no movement within, I turn the knob slowly and ease the door open with bated breath.

I needn't have worried. Jake is sound asleep, balled under the covers. His face is slack, and his chest rises and falls evenly. With only the moonlight to guide me, I glance around the room. Surely, he must have his phone in here somewhere?

I find it sitting on the bedside table. The screen is dark. I gingerly reach over and lift it, moving as slowly and quietly as I can. I don't want the phone to light up and wake Jake, not when I'm so close to obtaining the proof I so desperately need.

Luck is on my side. Jake doesn't even stir, and I manage to retreat out into the safety of the hallway, phone in hand, with him none the wiser.

I hate that this isn't the first time I've had to check his phone. There was that other... indiscretion... a few years ago now. Jake promised that I'd have full access to his devices if it would help me trust him again, and I've known his passwords ever since.

But I haven't gone this far in a long time. Now, guilt gnaws at me as I press the button that conjures up the phone's lock screen.

"That fucking little weasel," I hiss under my breath. Instead of the familiar array of numbers that usually pops up, there's a prompt for a thumbprint.

I'm locked out.

Unless…

My resolve coalesces into a small, bright diamond. I won't have any peace until I know the truth. If I wait until tomorrow and demand that Jake unlock his phone, he might simply refuse. Plus, he'd already have had time to go through his device and delete anything incriminating.

No, it has to be now.

Steeling myself, I slip back into the guest room. Jake hasn't moved. My heart pounds in my chest as I inch forward. When I'm close enough, I take a risk and light up the lock screen.

Jake's eyelids flutter, but he doesn't wake up. I want to sigh in relief, but I'm afraid to make a single sound.

Slowly, I hold the phone in front of one of his unmoving hands. This is going to be the hardest part. Using the softest touch I can muster, I gingerly take his thumb and shift it ever so slightly forward. It seems to take forever before the pad of his fingers brushes against the screen.

The lock screen disappears, revealing a sea of apps.

Thank fucking goodness.

I slide the phone away from him as carefully as possible and then tiptoe out of the room. Easing the door shut, I retrace my steps back downstairs to the living room.

Sitting on the couch with my legs tucked underneath me, I get to work. I check his text messages first, but they all seem innocuous. There's a thread between him and me, of course. A pang of irritation reverberates through me as I realize he's listed me in his contacts only as WIFE. The other contacts all look to be business related, which doesn't come as much of a surprise.

Frustrated, I exit out of the app and switch to his email. There's nothing there either. A closer inspection reveals that he doesn't even have any other messaging apps, dating sites, or any social media other than the clean accounts I already know about.

"What the fuck am I doing?" I sigh as I stare down at the phone, willing it to spill its secrets. But what do I expect, that the universe will align, and some random woman will call him right now, asking for sex?

It takes me a second before I realize I haven't actually checked his call log. And while I don't really expect anything to be there, I have nothing else to lose now that I've gone this far.

I hit the app and am instantly faced with a list of names and numbers. I recognize some of them, and most seem to have to do with his business dealings, but the most recent call stands out to me. It's a phone number with no name attached, and the log shows that Jake dialed it right after he stormed upstairs.

Dread churns inside of me as I hover my finger over the number. Part of me wants to just lock the phone and put it back like nothing ever happened. But the doubt of not knowing will eat me alive. I have no choice.

I dial the number.

The phone rings a few times before somebody picks up.

"Hey, sugar," a woman's voice purrs across the line. "Calling for seconds?"

Anger, grief, and vindication instantly hurtle through me, each fighting for dominance over the others. My stomach clenches, and I suddenly feel like the few bites of food I'd eaten earlier are going to resurrect themselves in a most inelegant fashion.

"Jake?" the woman asks. "Are you there?"

"This isn't Jake," I say. My voice sounds fragile, small. "This is his wife."

The stranger is silent. I listen for any indication that she's hung up, and just when I think she won't answer at all, she gasps, "Oh my God, I swear I didn't know he was married!"

I'm not sure that I believe her, but it's not like it even matters. "Who are you?" I demand. I want a name, something concrete I can throw back in Jake's face later.

"Ellie," she replies tentatively. "I *thought* I was Jake's girlfriend."

"And how long have you thought that?" I force out through gritted teeth. I want to scream at this woman, this home wrecker, but I also know one catch more flies with honey than vinegar.

Ellie pauses for only a moment. "Six months? Ever since he moved to Louisiana. He visits me when he's in the city for work."

The tears that threatened to fall earlier make themselves known once again, stinging at the corner of my eyes. I blink hard, willing them back. I will *not* cry on the phone with this lady. I won't give her, or Jake, the satisfaction.

I just need to keep it together for my last question.

"Did he visit you today?"

"Yes, ma'am," she murmurs demurely. "And he called a little while ago, if you know what I mean." She draws in a shaky breath, and I get the impression that she wants me to think she's distraught rather than genuinely upset. "Honestly, I didn't know. I'm so..."

I hang up before she can finish the sentence.

Cold rage drives me as I stomp back upstairs and throw the door to the guest room open. It thuds against the wall, and Jake shoots up in bed at the loud noise.

"Julia?" he croaks, his voice crackling with sleep. "What the fuck are you doing?"

"What the fuck am *I* doing?" I snarl. "What the fuck are *you* doing? Or should I say, *who the fuck are you doing?*" I hold the unlocked phone up, revealing the call I'd just made.

Jake scrambles up out of bed. "Did you go through my fucking phone?" he parries. It's bait, and I don't take it.

"What's her name, Jake?" I press, my volume rising.

"What? Who? I don't know who you're talking about!"

"Oh, should I call Ellie back and tell her you forgot her fucking name?"

Horror passes over Jake's features as he realizes that I know. But it's quickly replaced by anger and something else, something darker. His eyes flash, and for a shard of a section, his face seems to writhe and change, like bugs are crawling beneath his skin.

And then he raises his hand and slaps me.

The crack of the impact seems to echo through the guest room. Pain explodes in my cheek, radiating up through the fine bones of my face and into my eye socket.

Jake's features churn once more before they settle into a mask of shock and regret.

For a moment, time stands still. There's a gaping, silent chasm between us, one that I fear can never be bridged.

I bring my hand to my face, wincing as pain throbs beneath my fingers.

The small motion seems to snap Jake out of it. He reaches for me, but I shy away.

"Don't you fucking touch me," I hiss. I don't think I could bear it if he did.

He flinches like a wounded animal. "Julia?" His voice is broken and empty, no longer powerful. "Julia, I…I don't…I…"

Adrenaline pumps through my veins as I back away from him, moving slowly but steadily toward the door. A mess of emotions, none of them good, rise and fall inside of me, twisting my nerves into knots. But my body understands what my mind will not, that no matter what Jake says now, I know I'm in danger.

I stumble backward out the door and into the hallway. I keep my eyes on Jake until he's lost from view, and then I turn and flee. Half blinded by tears and pain, I stagger down the stairs and into our bedroom.

Heavy footfalls behind me alert me that Jake is in pursuit. "Julia, please! Wait!" he calls from halfway down the stairs.

I throw myself into the bedroom, slamming the door and locking it behind me.

Jake slides to a halt in front of the threshold. His shadow creeps in under the door as he tries the knob only to find it securely locked.

"Julia, I'm sorry. Please, honey, let me in," he begs.

"Go away!" I cry. I can't keep the tears from falling now. They streak down my face, stinging the sensitive flesh of my wounded cheek.

"Please," he pleads. He sounds pathetic, like a child. How could I have married this man? "Please, let me in so we can talk. I'm sorry. I'm so sorry. It was like I wasn't even myself for a minute. You have to believe me!"

This time, I don't answer. I just stand there, staring at the shadow of his legs on the other side of the door. And then finally, after several minutes pass, he retreats back up to the third floor.

My legs don't feel like they can hold me any longer, so I drag myself over to the bed and fall onto the mattress. I curl up into a ball and train my eyes on the perfect white plaster of the ceiling.

What Jake just did is unforgivable, far worse than the cheating. In all of the years we've been together, he's been mean, petty, and dishonest. He's sullied our fidelity and has failed to satisfy me. But not once has he ever raised a hand against me.

Until now.

I think about how his face looked when he hit me. It seemed twisted and unnatural, wholly inhuman. Is that what Jake looks like inside, underneath the charm, the body, and the piles of money? Is he nothing more than a monster wearing the skin of a man?

A sob wracks my body, and I squeeze my eyes shut.

There will be no peace for me tonight.

Maybe there will never be peace again.

10
REPERCUSSIONS

Jake

Oh God, what have I done?

Panic and desperation crash over me in unrelenting tidal waves, dragging me under until I'm drowning in them. I'm sitting on the bed in the guest room, holding my head in my hands and rocking back and forth.

I don't know how long I've been here. Hours, probably. At some point, I'd stumbled down to the kitchen to grab a bottle of whiskey. It sits on the floor by my feet, the amber liquid significantly drained.

The alcohol hadn't helped. I'm unable to numb the tumult that roils inside of me.

I hit my wife.

She deserved it.

The cold, foreign voice slithers through my mind, and I groan, trying to drown it out.

I've done a lot of questionable things over the years, some more legal than others. And maybe, just maybe, I'd said things to intentionally hurt Julia in the past, but I'd never physically harmed her.

Until tonight.

She was asking for it.

"Shut up!" I whimper, clawing at my temples. "Shut up!"

I stand and start pacing in the small space between the bed and the window in a weak attempt to distract myself. On one pass, my bare foot hits the bottle of whiskey. The hefty glass vessel teeters and falls, spilling the spirit out onto the beige carpet. I make no attempt to stop it from spilling or clean it up. Judging by the way the world is swimming around me, I've probably already had enough to drink.

As the sharp scent of alcohol fills the space, the room begins to feel more and more claustrophobic, as though the walls are closing in. I stumble to the window and throw the sash open before sticking my head out into the humid night air.

I draw in a few gulping breaths. The scent of the swamp curls around me, accompanied by a chorus of insects singing in the brush. The storm has lulled, and now there's only a gentle pattering of rain on the roof. The drops are cool and refreshing, and I blink against them like a newborn seeing the sun for the first time.

My mind clears a bit more as the seconds tick by, and my eyes adjust to the darkness. I stare out at the driveway down below, and a sense of déjà vu slides over me. Isn't this where that contractor fell and broke his back during construction? I think it was.

Unbidden, the skin on the back of my neck prickles to life as I imagine what it must have felt like for the man when he'd realized that he was at the mercy of gravity and nothing more. If I'm remembering correctly, there was even a rumor that the guy claimed he was pushed, though I never put much stock into it.

My eyes trail over the gravel where the worker landed before sweeping over to the garage. To my shock, the door, which had been completely shut after the whole car incident, is open.

"Fuck," I mutter. I'm absolutely sure that the door closed, albeit on its own. Maybe there was some sort of electrical malfunction. Either way, I can't just leave it open. Who knows what kind of wildlife might crawl in out of the muck of the swamp? The rain alone is bad enough, but there will be hell to pay if I go out to find little muddy paw prints all over my precious cars.

I lean back into the room and close the window. Sidestepping the growing puddle of whiskey that mars the carpet, I snatch my phone off the bedside table and make my way out of the room.

The hallway is dark and quiet. Even as I descend the stairs and pass by our bedroom, the shadows remain still. A thin crack of light spills from under the door, but there's no sound coming from within. I wonder if Julia has fallen asleep or if she's just lying there, thinking about what I did to her.

Shame washes over me as I slink past the threshold and down toward the ground floor. I hadn't meant to hit her. I really hadn't. It felt like somebody else jumped into my body, if only for a split second. It was as if I was a puppet, as if the rage I'd felt in that moment wasn't my own.

But I'd felt the sting in my hand when my palm connected with the soft skin of Julia's delicate cheek, and that pain was mine and nobody else's.

The sound of my hand against her face rings in my memory, playing back again and again in my mind's eye. Did it hurt her? Or were those tears from shock? Did it left a mark? God, I don't think I can face her if she ends up with a bruise. I don't want a physical reminder of what I did every time I look at her.

When I reach the front door, I turn on my phone's flashlight before stepping out into the dreary night. The light doesn't do much, but it's better than nothing as I step gingerly across the driveway. Gravel bites into my bare feet, and I stumble several times over ruts and potholes. Finally, I reach the garage and duck inside.

Everything is exactly as I'd left it earlier. The car gleams in the low beam of the phone's flashlight. Lucky for me, it doesn't look like it's dirty, but I decide to check again in the morning once it's light out.

Satisfied that there's nothing wrong, I hit the button for the garage door and step back out into the rain through the side door so I don't signal the door to stop.

Nothing happens.

I reach inside and slap the button again, but the door doesn't budge. Even after a third, harder attempt, there's no change.

"For fuck's sake," I groan. Why did the garage door opener have to give up the ghost tonight? Why couldn't it have chosen a better fucking time? I consider going back inside and dealing with it tomorrow, but the thought of leaving the door open and exposing the vehicle to the elements for so long doesn't sit right with me.

Resigning myself to my fate, I step back inside the garage and make a beeline over to the stepladder leaning against the wall. I drag it over and fold it open underneath the door. I figure I'll yank the door down just far enough for me to reach it from the ground, put the ladder away, and then close it the rest of the way from outside.

The metal of the stepladder is cold and gritty beneath my naked soles. I register dimly that I probably shouldn't be doing this when I'm drunk, but I quickly push the thought aside. I'm climbing a ladder, for fuck's sake, not Mount Everest. It'll be fine. It'll only take a minute.

I balance on the top step, swaying from the alcohol in my system. I reach up as high as I can until my fingers brush the edge of the garage door. Catching the lip of it, I pull down.

The ladder rattles underneath me. For a moment, I'm simply confused, but then the surface is yanked out from under me and I'm flying.

I land on my back on the damp concrete. Air rushes from my lungs on impact as the wind is knocked out of me. I find the ladder with wild eyes, trying to figure out what happened.

For a split second, I swear that there's an old lady standing next to the toppled stepladder. There's a triumphant smile on her face. But then I blink, and she's gone.

I really must be fucking drunk.

Gasping for air, I manage to sit up. One shoulder aches in protest, and I think dismally that Julia isn't going to be the only one with a bruise tomorrow.

Once I'm able to stand, I decide that I've had enough of ladders for one night. The garage door can stay open. If a raccoon gets inside and shits on my car, so be it.

I stagger out into the night. It isn't until I'm halfway back to the house that I realize that something isn't right.

It's completely silent.

Though I can still feel the gentle drizzle of rain against my skin, it makes no noise against the leaves or the ground. The insects have ceased their chatter, and even the leaves seem to be holding their breath.

Goosebumps crawl across my skin as I get the distinct impression that somebody is watching me.

I spin on my heel, sending up a spray of gravel. "Who's there?" I call toward the swamp.

There's no reply.

I squint toward the tree line, trying to make out any discernible shapes. At first glance, there's nothing there. But then a shadow detaches from the rest, and I realize that I'm looking at the outline of a man.

"Hello?" I shout again. My voice seems so loud against the silence.

The figure raises one hand and beckons me to approach.

Angrily, I pick my way across the driveway, only lengthening my stride as the gravel shifts to the soft grass of the back yard. Fear eats at me with every step, but I feel compelled forward, as though there's a rope reeling me in like I'm nothing more than a fish on a line.

When I'm close enough to see the man's face, terror overpowers my momentum, and I stop in my tracks.

I recognize this guy. It's the head contractor who built the house, the one who went crazy and disappeared. What was his name again? Tyson? Tyler?

He smiles at me, and the blood freezes in my veins. Even though he looks human, there's something off about his smile, as though he'd been fashioned out of mud and painted to look like a person.

Whoever this is, I don't think it's the builder.

I think this is the thing that drove that guy crazy in the first place.

"Good evening, Jake." The thing greets me in a voice like the wind through the cypress trees.

There is nothing good about this evening, but I'm not about to tell this creature that. Feeling like I'm going to piss myself at any second, I manage to stammer, "What... what are you?"

The thing's grin widens. "Call me Amos," it slithers. "All my friends do. And I think you and I are going to be very good friends. Don't you?"

It's all I can do to shake my head no.

A parody of a pout stretches across its face. For the first time, I notice its eyes are matte black. "But I could give you so much, Jake. Power, money, prowess. Anything you've ever wanted could be yours."

"Yeah, right," I scoff.

"You doubt me?" it questions, cocking its head. "You can sense it, can't you? I have the power, Jake. Reality bends to me."

It waves one hand, and we're no longer standing in the rain at the edge of the swamp. Instead, I'm standing in a spotless modern office overlooking the New York City skyline. A huge desk dominates the space, and written on the placard beneath the title CEO is my name.

"Isn't this what you want?" Amos purrs as it gestures to the grand space.

I nod, too blown away to even try to form words.

"You work so hard, Jake, and you've been quite successful, but you haven't made it big yet, have you? All you need is a push in the right direction." It gestures again, and the scene melts away.

"Why me?" I ask, no longer doubting this thing's ability.

"Because you have something I want," it grins. "Something special."

My mind flickers through the many items I own, but I can't think of anything that Amos could possibly want. After all, what could I offer that it couldn't just conjure for itself?

"What is it?" I press. "What do you want in return?"

Amos' eyes sparkle in the darkness. "Julia."

And then he's gone, leaving me alone in the darkness to consider his terrible offer.

The fate of my wife rests in my hands.

11

STOLEN KISS

Zeke

Something dreadful happened last night.

I'd been out in the swamp, enjoying the sound of the rain pattering off the soft fronds of the ferns in the underbrush when I'd noticed Jake stumbling drunkenly to the garage.

Even worse, I watched from the shadows as he spoke to that *thing* as though he was just making another shady business deal. Though I wasn't able to hear what Amos demanded, I think I have a pretty good idea what it is.

Who it is.

I watched Jake stagger around the property for a while before he got into his car and drove off. Good riddance, in my opinion.

But I'm concerned for Julia. I don't trust Jake for a second, and she doesn't deserve to be used as a pawn in this sick game.

And now I'm lingering at her front door, my hand raised and poised to press the doorbell. For a moment, I don't think I can go through with it, but then the memory of Jake speaking with Amos flashes through my mind, and I know I have no other option. I have to make sure she's all right.

Thinking about how I'd taken the coffee cup from Julia the other morning, I close my eyes and push my index finger against the button.

Two chimes ring out inside the house, announcing my presence.

After a moment, I hear the bustle of somebody on the stairs and the slide of the lock. Then the door swings open, revealing Julia.

"Zeke?" she gasps, clearly surprised to see me.

She's wearing a rumpled dress that looks like it's been slept in, and her feet are bare. Her hair is disheveled, and instead of her usually proud posture, her shoulders sag in weary defeat. She's holding her head oddly to one side, as though she's trying to hide her face from me.

Concern ripples through me as I take in her haggard appearance, but it's quickly overruled by anger as I notice the cloudy bruise forming on her cheekbone and around her eye.

"Are you okay?" I blurt out, unable to drag my gaze away from her marred skin. "Who did this to you?"

Julia shakes her head. "It's nothing," she breathes. I can tell that she's teetering on the verge of tears.

"That's not nothing," I insist, lifting my hand. I expect her to flinch away from me, but instead she leans forward slightly, as though she too craves to close the distance between us. The calloused skin of my fingertips ghosts over her cheekbone. At my touch, her eyelids flutter closed, and a small sigh forms across her lips.

The feel of her is electric. It glides through my veins and sings across my nerves, a lightning storm in a bottle.

"Jake did this, didn't he?" I ask, my voice soft and low. Rage bubbles below the surface, but I don't unleash it. I won't, not at Julia.

She nods, her eyes drifting downward in shame. But she has nothing to be ashamed of. The guilt lies with Jake, not her. He's the monster who did this to her. And with a sinking feeling, I wonder what else he's done and what he still might do.

"Would you like some coffee?" Julia asks meekly. Her eyes still won't meet mine.

"Yes, please," I reply. She steps inside, and I follow her, shutting the door firmly behind us before she leads the way to the kitchen.

Silence reigns as Julia moves on autopilot toward the fancy coffee machine. "Let me," I offer, gesturing to the contraption. I'm not exactly sure how it works, but I'm certain I can figure it out.

"Thanks." Smiling thinly, she slides onto one of the stools at the island.

As I fumble with the coffee machine, I can feel her eyes on my back. After a few seconds of trying to figure out where, precisely, the coffee grounds are supposed to go, Julia takes pity on me.

"Why don't we have tea instead?" she suggests.

Offering her a sheepish grin, I grab the kettle, fill it with water, and place it on the stove. She points to a cupboard, where I find mugs and several boxes of tea bags. I fish out two bags of earl grey and plop them into a pair of matching cups.

While the kettle boils, I perch on the stool beside her. "Do you want to talk about it?" I ask. We both know what I mean.

Julia blinks rapidly, and I realize that she's trying desperately not to cry. "What's to talk about?" she murmurs. "Jake hit me."

Even though she previously confirmed it already, just hearing those words tumble from her mouth lights a fire in my chest. I want to face Jake, to make him feel as small as he made her feel. I want to hurt him, scare him.

But I don't want to frighten Julia, so I ask again, "What happened?"

She finally turns to look at me. Her brilliant green eyes glisten with unshed tears, and her bottom lip quivers as she speaks. "He's cheating on me. I… I think I've known for a while, but I got proof yesterday." She draws in a shaky breath before continuing, "I checked his phone. I knew he was lying about going on all of those business trips, and it turns out he's been with another woman the whole fucking time!"

A sob escapes her then as emotion overtakes her. Emboldened by our earlier contact, I reach out and place one large hand on her back.

She stills for a moment before melting into my touch. With her silent permission, I begin to trace soothing circles between her shoulder blades.

"I confronted him," she laments. "And he…. It was like he was another person. A monster."

Anger seethes inside of me as I press, "Is this the first time he's hit you?"

The small nod of her head offers little relief. "I don't know what to do. I thought about calling the police, but… I just can't. Besides, I don't even know where he is. Probably with *her*," she spits bitterly. "I don't understand what I did wrong."

I nearly come unglued at her words. "Wrong? You did nothing wrong, Julia," I tell her earnestly. "He cheated on you and hit you. None of that is your fault. It's his. Jake doesn't deserve you, and you deserve somebody who treats you with respect and dignity."

I'm not sure if I've said the right thing or the wrong thing. Either way, Julia erupts into a fresh bout of sobs and all but flings herself into my arms. I hold her tight, relishing the feel of her body against mine.

It's a foolish, wicked thought, but I can't help it. Ever since I first laid eyes on her, she's haunted me. And now, she's looking to me for comfort after her rake of a husband abused her. I try to tell myself this is wrong, that I shouldn't be here holding her, but her presence is too intoxicating. The weight of her against me, the smell of her hair as she hides her bruised face against my neck, it drives me wild.

Knowing that she's in pain is nearly unbearable. All I want to do is to take it away for her, to take care of her. But I can't.

I can't.

Closing my eyes, I lean into our embrace, savoring this moment.

The whistle of the kettle splits the silence, and Julia jumps back as though she's been burned.

"I'm so sorry," she mumbles as a red flush creeps across her face.

"You have nothing to apologize for," I insist. Not wanting to make her feel any more awkward, I stand and pour the hot water into the mugs. By the time I turn back around, Julia's composed herself once again. She's staring down at her wedding ring, twisting it around and around on her finger.

"Thank you," she says as I slide one of the mugs over to her. She picks it up and clinks it against mine. "Cheers," she toasts dryly. "To the end of my marriage."

"So you're going to divorce him, then?" I'd been worried that she wouldn't have the strength to leave him, but the thought of her getting rid of Jake for good makes my heart flutter traitorously against my ribs.

"I should have the first time he cheated," she grumbles. "He said it was a mistake. Promised he wouldn't do it again. All lies, of course. Comfortable fucking lies."

"He's a scoundrel," I confirm.

Julia huffs out a laugh and turns on her stool to face me. "A scoundrel? What is this, Victorian England?" It's good to hear some humor back in her voice. Her emerald eyes fix on mine, studying me.

Whatever she's looking for, she seems to find it.

Moving slowly, as though she might scare me away, she leans forward. My breath hitches in my throat as I realize what's about to happen.

I shouldn't. I know I shouldn't.

But my body moves before my brain can catch up, and suddenly my lips are on hers.

Julia sinks into the kiss. As our mouths move as one, I feel the brush of her breasts against my chest when she shifts closer. I skim one hand down to the tantalizing curve of her hip while the other cups her cheek gently, coaxing her to deepen the kiss.

Her hands card into my hair, and when I feel the insistent drag of her manicured nails against my scalp, I can't help but groan against her mouth. She gasps at my reaction, and I take the opportunity to dart my tongue out and taste her. She meets me willingly, drawing me closer as she shifts halfway onto my lap.

At the feel of her pressing against my hips, my cock twitches to life.

Julia freezes.

For a moment, neither of us moves. There's no sound except for the ragged panting of our mingled breath. Julia's eyes are still closed, her expression unreadable.

After a few more agonizing seconds, she slides off of my lap and takes several steps back. Her lips are swollen from our kiss, and her eyes are glassy with emotion.

"I'm sorry," she murmurs. "You… you'd better go."

I blink at her. Did I misread her intentions?

"Please," she whispers, closing her eyes once again.

I don't say anything. I rise from the island and exit the kitchen, and she doesn't make any attempt to follow me as I let myself out the front door.

I stand out in the sunlight, disbelief and uncertainty racing through me. I raise my fingers to my lips, chasing the ghost of Julia's mouth against mine. Did that really just happen?

Did Julia and I really just kiss?

A seed of guilt blooms deep within my gut. I should have had better control over myself. After all, what future could she and I possibly have? Even if she does leave Jake, she can never be mine.

I'm so lost in my thoughts that I barely notice the shape of the elderly woman coalescing by my side. It isn't until the shade speaks that she catches my attention.

"Did she tell you what her husband did to her last night?" she asks, nodding back toward the house. I know she's talking about Julia, even if she doesn't say her name.

I nod.

"That boy wasn't raised right," she sighs. "I helped him along though."

"You did?" I ask, raising a questioning eyebrow.

"I opened the garage door and got rain all over his precious car. Honey, he treats that thing better than his own wife. And when he got up on the ladder to fix it, I kicked it right out from under him."

"Well played, Miss Penny," I chuckle.

"Laying a hand on Miss Julia and running around on her, now that's no way to treat a lady," the ghost huffs.

"Damn right," I agree.

"Speaking of which, I expect you to mind your manners with her, Zeke," she warns. "When are you going to tell her truth?"

The truth.

The reason there's no future for us.

"I don't know," I sigh, guilt rising up within me once again.

Miss Penny fixes me with a disapproving frown. "You need to tell her, Zeke, before either of you get hurt."

I can't tell her it's already too late, that my heart's already aflame.

12

THE MAN IN THE GARAGE

JULIA

I CAN'T STAY HERE.

Jake's been gone all day. In fact, I hadn't even heard him leave in the first place, and God only knows where he went. But I'm absolutely sure that I don't want to be here when he gets back.

If he comes back.

Would that really be so bad, I wonder? It's true that I hate it out here at the edge of the festering swamp, locked away in this big empty house with only ghosts for company. But without Jake tying me down, I could go anywhere, do anything.

I could even find another man, one who would treat me better than the bastard I'd married.

A fine blush rises in my cheeks as the memory of Zeke's passion whispers across my lips. Guilt trickles through me in its wake. I can't believe we'd kissed. As terrible as Jake's actions have been, I've never once felt the need to seek out another man.

But there is something about Zeke that beckons me, drawing me closer like a lighthouse in the dark. It isn't just that he's handsome, or even that he's nice to me. I have the uncanny, uncomfortable feeling that we are tethered somehow. Every time we touch, that certainty has only grown, and it's become so strong that I can barely stand it.

I have to get out of here.

Moving with renewed energy, I scurry into the bathroom to retrieve some toiletries. I set the bag down on top of the neatly folded piles of clothes and then zip the duffel shut. I've only packed the essentials, knowing that I can always buy whatever extras I need once I reach my destination.

After Zeke left, I finally caved and called Nina. Though I'd feared that my best friend would gloat that she told me so, she was nothing short of kind and understanding. She suggested, without hesitation, that I should come and stay in her guest room in her New York City penthouse, and I accepted her generous offer just as readily.

The thought of getting into one of Jake's fancy cars and speeding away from this wretched place and the stench of the swamp is the only thing driving me at this point.

I heft the duffel bag onto my shoulder, grab my handbag, and flee.

Stepping out of the house is a relief. Freedom is just around the corner, and nothing can stop me now.

But then, as I round the bed of one of the worker's trucks, I nearly bump into a man who must have been leaning against the vehicle.

I turn to him, ready to apologize, but the words die in my throat as my eyes lock on his.

On the surface, I recognize him. It's Tanner, the guy who built the house. What did people say about him? That he lost his mind and kidnapped his girlfriend or something?

There's something off about him, though I can't quite put my finger on it. He's oddly still, and his expression seems frozen some-how, like a person in a stock photo.

"Can I help you?" I finally find my voice. As far as I know, Tanner shouldn't be here. Maybe the guys working in the cemetery needed him for something?

The contractor's expression doesn't change, and when he speaks, his mouth moves like a poorly wrought mask. "Going somewhere?"

he asks. His voice has a strange quality to it. It reminds me of the high-pitched buzz of the insects that hum every evening in the marsh. The tone is so grating that it makes my fillings hurt.

"That's none of your business," I snap, narrowing my eyes. Is this really Tanner? It's been almost a year since I last saw him, and I quite liked him at that time. Perhaps this is some random guy who's wandered in off the street who only just resembles the construction worker. "Why are you here?" I press, wanting to get to the bottom of this so I can get the hell out of here.

"To work," he says simply.

"On what, exactly?"

"The house."

I stare at him uneasily. I'm not aware of anything structurally wrong or broken, not that I've been paying much attention. But maybe Jake called him here for something. Hadn't he mentioned that the garage door was acting wonky?

Either way, it doesn't matter. I can feel my resolve crumbling with each passing second. If I don't leave now, I'm afraid that my doubt will overtake me. So I tell the builder tersely, "This isn't a good time."

"It is," Tanner insists as he straightens to his full height. A prickle of fear skitters down my spine, and I take a step back from him. Even though I can't put my finger on it, something feels wrong here.

Tanner smiles, and it's like something from a horror movie, subtle but deeply disturbing. I don't even know why his expression instills such terror in me.

He steps around me and walks with an odd, jilting gait toward the garage. My heart sinks as I realize that all of the cars are parked in there, and I won't be able to leave without trapping myself inside the outbuilding with Tanner.

I'm stuck.

Once the contractor is out of sight, my fear flares into white hot anger. Did Jake do this on purpose? Did he summon Tanner out here to do some bogus work on the garage to stop me from leaving?

I know my judgment is clouded by my emotions right now, but I can't stop myself from pulling my phone out and jabbing at the screen, dialing Jake's number. The phone barely rings before my sorry excuse for a husband picks up.

"Julia?" he breathes. His voice sounds unsteady, and I suspect he's been drinking. Hell, I can practically smell the fumes over the phone. "Baby, I'm sorry. You gotta believe me," he slurs.

"Do you think this is funny?" I hiss. "Sending the contractor out so I wouldn't leave you?"

My words are met with several seconds of stunned silence before he finds his voice. "Who? I dunno what you're talking about."

"The contractor," I snap, enunciating every syllable. "Tanner. He's here saying he needs to work on the garage."

"The garage?" Jake parrots.

"Yes, you know, the little square building where you park your cars." It's all I can do not to scream with frustration.

"I know what the fucking garage is," he grumbles over the line. "Why though?"

An uncanny feeling settles in the pit of my stomach. Jake isn't exactly a paragon of honesty, but he's a terrible liar when he's drunk. I have to know for sure, though. "You didn't call him?" I ask.

"Why would I?" he retorts before a thought seems to occur to him. "Wait, did you?"

"No," I utter. Before he can say another word, I quickly add, "I've got to go."

He starts to reply, but I end the call there. I've already got all the information I need. The last thing I want is to listen to him stumble over yet another drunken apology.

Anxiety floods through me as I glance over at the garage. The automatic door is open, and I can just vaguely make out the shape of Tanner looming in the darkness. He doesn't appear to be doing anything. He's just… staring. Watching.

Waiting.

In spite of the cloying heat of the day, I shiver. I certainly didn't call Tanner out here. And if Jake hadn't either, then who did?

Drowning under the weight of the contractor's unmoving stare, I decide to go back inside. But even as I step into the cool air conditioned front hallway and drop my bags at the bottom of the stairs, it feels like he's still looming just over my shoulder.

I really don't want to be here. I feel like a trapped animal, pacing in its cage. I can't leave, not with Tanner lurking like a giant creep out in the garage. But if I stay in this house, I'm going to go crazy.

Zeke's face flashes through my mind, stirring up the familiar warmth in my lower belly. Is he still here, I wonder? I'd seen the work crew's trucks out in the driveway. If he is, I bet he's out in the swamp getting the last of the graves dug up.

The thought of venturing out into the marsh isn't exactly pleasant, but at least I'll have some company.

My mind made up, I kick off my heels and instead slip into a pair of sensible sneakers before retreating to the back door. As soon as I step out onto the porch, I'm enveloped by the comforting sounds of casual banter and the growl of power tools. I stride across the lawn, doing my best not to look over my shoulder toward the back of the garage.

At the edge of the swamp, I pause, suddenly doubting my plan. It's muddy. Like, *really* muddy. The treacherous ground gives the impression that the stagnant pools of water are much deeper than they appear. The smell of the mire is so thick in the soupy air that I can practically taste it. As I linger, the gnarled branches of the cypress trees beckon to me with twisted fingers, the leaves whispering amongst themselves.

Swallowing back my trepidation, I take a step into the swamp.

Muck pulls at my sneaker, but my foot doesn't sink. It's not so bad. I take another tentative stride forward, and when I'm not immediately slurped down into the depths of the muck, I start to move more confidently. I pick my way between mossy rocks and tree trunks until I finally haul myself up onto the bleak little island that houses the cemetery.

"Howdy, ma'am," the foreman greets, offering a polite hand to steady me as I find my footing on the solid ground. He seems surprised that I've waded all the way out here. "What brings you to our neck of the woods?"

I can't exactly say that I've come to ogle one of his workers, so instead, I ignore the question and ask, "Did you call a contractor out?"

Confusion passes over the foreman's expression. "No, ma'am," he says. "Why? Do you need a recommendation? I know a great guy out of NOLA who might be willing to come down, but nobody closer."

I shake my head. "Thank you, but no. I was just curious." I risk a nervous glance toward the house. The building looms over the tops of the trees and blots out the sky, but the sight lines toward the driveway and garage are spotty at best. Although I can't spot him, I can feel the intensity of Tanner's gaze boring into my skin.

The foreman shrugs. "If you'd asked me a year ago, I'd have said you should call Tanner. Best in the business, if you ask me. But he up and went to Florida with that cute nurse of his, and now there ain't nobody willing to help out around these parts."

"You mean, Tanner really did leave town?" I press.

Dread fills me at the man's answer. "Yep. He left before finishing this place, actually. Swore he'd never come back to Hahnville."

"Why?" I try to keep my tone even, but I'm more alarmed than I let on. If the contractor isn't even in the state, and nobody called him, then who the hell is currently in the garage?

The older man shakes his head. "I ain't gonna lie to you, ma'am. This swamp's a strange place. I'm sure you've heard the stories by now." He glances around uncomfortably, as though desperate to change the subject. "Anyhow, I won't go scaring you with those stories. Besides, you'll be rid of the marsh soon enough." He points over at his crew. "We've only got two graves left, and then we'll get to work draining the swamp."

It's funny to think that this will all be part of the back lawn in a few short weeks. For months, I've waited for this news. But now, I just feel numb.

I don't want to stay here to see it.

I don't want to know what's lying on the bottom of the swamp.

I start to mentally check out as the foreman continues to chatter, explaining the process and gesturing to the areas they'll start with. As I nod along, my eyes wander back toward the house.

I've never really been out here before. Now, I can't help but notice that I can see directly inside some of the windows, including into our bedroom. My face reddens with embarrassment as I realize that anybody could have looked in and seen me unintentionally putting on a show.

Vowing to close all of the blinds the second I go back inside, my gaze strays down to the yard.

My heart flutters as I catch sight of Zeke. He's standing on the edge of the grass, his back to the swamp. His stance is wide, and his shoulders are tense, as though he's fighting with somebody.

Desperately wanting to run over to him, I turn to the foreman, and cutting him off mid-sentence, I say, "I'm sorry, but I have to go."

But when I turn back toward the house, Zeke is gone.

Weird. I could swear he'd been there a second ago. A strange, heavy feeling settles in my gut, one I can't quite identify.

A large hand closes over my shoulder, and I jump. For a split second I think it must be Tanner, but then I realize it's just the foreman.

"You okay, ma'am?" he asks, concern creasing over his features.

"I'm fine," I lie.

The man fixes me with a scrutinizing stare. "Are you sure?" he presses. "You look like you've just seen a ghost."

I shake my head.

The only thing haunting this place is the ghost of my marriage.

13
DEAL WITH THE DEVIL

Jake

I can't go home.

I can't face Julia.

Releasing a groan of frustration, I fall back onto the hotel bed and stare, unseeing, at the lumpy patterns pockmarking the popcorn ceiling.

My stomach churns from dread and alcohol as my mind replays this afternoon's phone call with Julia. She sounded so cold, so detached. And she mentioned leaving, didn't she? I was already a few shots deep at the hotel bar, and now I can't quite remember the exact details of our conversation.

Seeing her contact pop up on my phone sent a teasing thrill of hope through me. Part of me hoped she'd be desperate at finding me gone and beg for me to come back. Instead, she asked about the builder and lectured me about the fucking garage.

Tears prick at the edges of my eyes, and I let them fall. I feel pathetic.

It's not the cheating that bothers me. We've done this before back in New York. I got too careless, too cocky. Julia found out and confronted me, but not like this. She was terrified of losing me. She would have said or done anything to get me to stay.

That's why I hit her, I worked out in my tequila-induced haze. I expected her to do the same thing as before, to grovel, beg, and prove to me why she is so valuable that I should stick around.

But this time, I feel like I have to prove to *her* that I am worth it.

How the fuck did that happen? How did Julia transform so completely under my nose, without me ever noticing until it was too late?

So it was her fault, really, that I hit her. She gave me no other choice.

No other choice.

That oozing, cold feeling wraps around my brain, working its way into the nooks and crannies. It's soothing somehow, almost comforting.

It understands me.

A small voice screams at me through the fog, urging me to wake up.

But I'm not sleeping.

Am I?

You're wide awake.

The eldritch voice is insistent, hard to push away. It's like a drug pumping slowly through my limbs, gradually at first, until my body is heavy and my mind is floating.

The light flickers, and the lumps of plaster on the ceiling seem to shift in the sudden onslaught of shadow. I squint up at them as they coalesce into something more recognizable.

A face.

A terrible, twisted face.

"Amos." I gasp hoarsely.

The image coalesces above me, almost solid but not quite. The thing's eyes gleam, and it reminds me of the way the moonlight occasionally reflects off of gators' eyes in the swamp. It's an animal—predatory.

Inhuman.

"What are you?" My mouth struggles to shape the words. It never occurred to me to ask before. How could I have ever thought it looked like the contractor or even like a person?

It grins, revealing thin, needle-like teeth. "Do you really want to know?"

I don't. I may be drunk, but I've got just enough hold over myself to know that this is the kind of knowledge you can never unlearn. But I find myself nodding anyway, and I have the vaguest sensation that it isn't me in charge of my body right now.

"I'm a demon," Amos reveals, its smile widening.

A high, demented laugh rolls from my lips.

I've never been a religious man. Church always got in the way of my Sunday morning hangovers, and I never put much stock into any of the stories about angels and devils or whatever.

But now, staring up at this monstrous thing, I realize that it can only be the truth.

"No," I try to say, as though denying the obvious would undo what the thing has told me, what is hovering right in front of my eyes. "There's no such thing."

"How rude," Amos smirks. It reaches one bony hand out until the curved nail taps my forehead. In a flash, I can feel it writhing inside my skull, serpentine, endless, and beyond my comprehension.

And then it's gone, and I'm left dry heaving on my back in the hotel bed as horror courses through my body.

"Do you believe me now?" it purrs.

I nod vigorously.

"And have you considered my offer?"

The offer. Anything I want—in exchange for Julia. I would never have considered that yesterday. But today? After that phone call? It's about time I teach her a lesson.

That small voice inside of me rises up once again, planting a seed of doubt in my mind. What am I doing? Am I seriously considering giving my wife to a demon?

"I... I can't," I stammer. "She's my wife."

Amos laughs, and the sound is like shattering glass. My hands slam against my ears as I wince against the sound, but it's inside my head. I can't block it out.

When it fades, the relief is as sweet as water in the desert. "What about a taste?" Amos suggests.

"A taste?" I repeat blankly.

"Yes, yes, only a taste," it assures me. "I know about your difficult investor. How would you like for him to call you with good news tomorrow?"

I recall the smug look the investor shot me after hesitating to back my project. It would be quite delicious to see him crawling back and offering me his capital.

The thought of it grants me enough confidence to ask, "And what do you want in return?"

Amos's grin grows impossibly wide. "I want to fuck your wife like I did that night when you first moved in. I want to impale her on my cock and feel her writhe beneath me until she's begging for her fucking life," it hisses.

A noxious mix of fear and anger hurtle through me at the revelation. I remember that feeling, that power, that coursed through my veins as I pounded into Julia that night. It was the best sex we ever had.

Amos was there, too, controlling me?

"Fuck you!" I howl at the ceiling. My limbs thrash against the scratchy hotel duvet, but my body is so heavy, and Amos is too far out of reach.

The thing laughs, and it's like all of the sounds of the swamp at once. "Do you hate me, Jake? You didn't seem to hate it then. All that power, all that virility. Don't you want to feel that again?"

That cold, damp feeling returns around my brain, poking and prodding me toward Amos. It was right, wasn't it? I *had* enjoyed fucking Julia like she was nothing more than an animal in heat. Would it really be so bad to give in to this? Hell, she probably wouldn't even know the difference.

"You can fuck my wife," I grind out, not giving myself the time to rethink my choice, "but you can't have total control."

"I see." Amos cocks its head at me, studying me as if it's deciding whether or not I'm serious.

"I want to feel it," I insist. Just thinking about Julia sinking down on my cock is getting me hard. I want to experience Amos's power running through me as I punish her for making me apologize, for making me hit her in the first place.

I want to teach her a fucking lesson.

A clacking noise summons me from my hedonistic thoughts. It takes me a moment to realize that it's the sound of Amos's claw-like nails clicking together in anticipation. Its eyes are bright and luminous, excited.

"I will give you nothing less," it promises.

"Then we have a deal."

"A deal!" it croons, clearly delighted. "You know, Jake, we have a lot in common, you and I."

Staring up at the thing on the ceiling, I doubt very highly that we share many similarities. But then I consider the fact that I essentially just whored out my wife for the sake of a business investment, and I realize that I can't exactly argue.

Part of me wants to take it back, though I don't think Amos would take kindly to that. Besides, there's something deep inside of me, buried under layers of money and charm, that's rotten.

I have my faults. I lie, I cheat, I do whatever I need to in order to get ahead. This is a business transaction, nothing more and nothing less. And isn't that what Amos is? Instead of real estate and construction, it deals in, well, deals.

"We just have one little problem." Amos's voice slithers through my consciousness, pulling me from my ruminations.

My heart thuds in my chest. What problem? And then I understand. It's Julia.

She hates me. She'd probably castrate me before letting me back into her bed.

"I have to apologize to her," I sigh. I don't want to. I shouldn't have to. And I hate her for it. "I'll have to convince her that I'm sorry."

"Are you?" Amos quizzes.

Yes.

No.

I scrub my hands over my face and groan in frustration. "What am I supposed to do?"

Amos regards me with those bright, livid eyes. "You play the part," it says. Its tone is a warning, a reminder not to fuck it up.

"How?" I spit bitterly.

A cruel smile twists the demon's lips. Its thin teeth glint in the swirling light of the room. "Pretend she's Ellie."

"Ellie?"

"The blonde," it chuckles. "The one you speak so sweetly to when your wife isn't listening."

Embarrassment and indignation war for dominance in my chest, but I push them down. Of course, Amos knows. "I'll do it," I force out through gritted teeth. "I'll get Julia back."

"You had better," Amos chides, the threat implicit in its voice. "A deal is a deal."

Squeezing my eyes shut, I nod. The alcohol gurgles up from my stomach, and I take a deep breath, forcing it to stay down. Once I'm feeling a bit calmer, I open my eyes again only to find that the light is back on, and the ceiling is once again just a plain lumpy surface.

Amos is gone, leaving me to do the impossible.

I struggle to sit up. The world swims around me for a moment as a wave of nausea rolls over me, but it passes quickly, and I manage to fish around for my cell phone.

For a moment, I toy with dialing Ellie. I'm pissed that she ratted me out to Julia, but the thought of her cunt sliding over my dick far outweighs my anger.

But what if Julia finds out somehow? Then I'll be really fucking screwed.

Fury seethes under the surface as I dial Julia's number. The phone seems to ring forever, each electronic chime ringing through my head like thunder.

But then she picks up, answering with that same frigid tone. "What?" she demands, not even bothering to greet me.

I draw in a deep breath and think about how I'll use her.

"Baby, I'm sorry," I beg. "Please, I want to come home and make this up to you. *Please.*"

Julia's silent for a moment.

It's the longest five seconds of my life.

14

TAKING WHAT'S HIS

Julia

As a great woman once said, diamonds are a girl's best friend.

I stand in front of the mirror in the trendy boutique in New Orleans, examining the new strand of precious stones adorning my throat. I'd paid for the mind-blowingly expensive necklace using Jake's platinum card, which had given me a small sliver of satisfaction.

He'd called in the early hours of the morning, begging for me to forgive him. At first, I'd told him that there was no way in hell I'd let him come crawling back to me, but all the while, my heart ached until the burn was almost unbearable.

One chance. That's all I'll give him.

In the meantime, I'll shamelessly spend down his accounts in preparation for the worst.

Because it would be terrible if we divorced, wouldn't it? I think wistfully of the lifestyle I've enjoyed over the last several years, excluding the months spent in solitude on the edge of a fetid swamp. I'd be losing much more than him if I left.

Doubt continues to gnaw at me as I gather my bags and head back to the car. I'd been so sure yesterday that leaving was my only option, but now I'm riddled with fear of the unknown. Maybe it won't be such a bad thing to hear Jake out.

After all, what am I afraid of?

That I'll forgive him?

A thrill of shame slides down my spine as I toss the bags into the passenger seat of one of Jake's flashy little sports cars. I know I shouldn't even consider it, not after he hit me.

"Get it together," I mutter to myself. I don't want him to see me rattled like this. Drawing in a deep breath, I force a veil of composure to drape over my features, obscuring the tempest that roils just beneath my skin.

The trip home seems to pass in a blink of an eye. A part of me wishes I'd hit terrible traffic somewhere between the city and Hahnville, but that would mean more time to wade through the troubled mess of my thoughts. That desire only intensifies as I emerge into the clearing of the driveway and catch sight of Jake's car parked in front of the house.

Resisting the urge to ram into the back of the vehicle, I instead pull up a few feet behind it, knowing that it will piss Jake off that I hadn't bothered to drive the few extra feet to the garage.

I've barely made it out of the car when the front door of the house flies open to reveal my husband.

At first glance, Jake's as put together as ever. He's wearing a pair of black slacks and a crisp button-up shirt in my favorite shade of emerald green. The sleeves are rolled to the elbow, revealing his muscled forearms. His hair is slicked back, reminding me of when we first started dating all those years ago.

But there's something in his eyes, something that reminds me of the way Tanner had looked earlier. It's like Jake's watching me like nothing else exists, like I'm prey.

A shiver runs through me, but I shake it off.

We stand for a moment, studying each other in tenuous silence. I watch as his gaze flickers over the curves of my body, outlined by the new dress I'd gotten in the city, before hovering at the diamonds lining my throat. A blush rises to my cheeks, and I'm the first to look away.

"Julia," he says after a long moment, drawing my eyes back to him. His voice is different from the desperate pleading of this morning. It's softer somehow, almost muted.

"Jake," I reply. I don't know how else to respond.

His posture breaks, and he runs a nervous hand through his hair. "I… I'm sorry."

I raise one eyebrow as the edges of my mouth quirk downward. He's going to have to do a lot better than that.

He nods, as though this is how he expected me to react. "I fucked up."

"Yes, you did," I agree. I cross my arms in front of my chest for emphasis.

If the barb wounds him, he doesn't argue. "The truth is, I've taken you for granted. When I first met you, I truly felt like I was the luckiest guy in the whole fucking world. But as time went on, I forgot to treat you like the beautiful, intelligent woman that you are. I failed you."

I want to repeat my former sentiment, but I hold it back. Jake is not the kind of man who makes earnest, heartfelt apologies. I've never once seen him self-reflect or take responsibility for his own actions. This new side of him is uncharted territory, and I suddenly feel uneasy, as though the ground could shift beneath me at any second and swallow me whole.

"When we grew distant in our marriage, I should have talked to you instead of… cheating." He yanks the word from his body with great difficulty. It only adds to my crawling sense of disquiet. "And then I… I hit you. I can't excuse that. I *won't*. You deserve better, and I understand that. If you choose to leave me, I won't fight it. But before you do, I have to ask for one more chance. Let me start over, like we're meeting for the first time. Let me do better. Let me *be* better."

He draws in one long, deep breath.

"Will you give me another chance?"

The question hangs in the humid air between us.

Something deep down inside me doubts that Jake will ever change. But I want to believe that it's possible, that I'm worth it to him.

What harm could one more chance do? If he fails me again, I'll leave. And if it works out, isn't that what I've wanted?

I close my eyes, fighting against reality and what I so desperately crave.

And then finally, I breathe out, "Okay."

"Okay?" Jake repeats, his voice barely rising above a whisper. The word is laced with awe, as though he can't quite believe what he's hearing.

Opening my eyes, I'm surprised to see that he's tearing up. "One last chance," I confirm. "Show me that you mean it."

"Thank you," he murmurs. He takes a step forward, raising his arms for an embrace, but I shift subtly away, my heels clacking against the gravel. If he's disheartened by my cue, he doesn't show it. Instead he tells me, "I've made us dinner. It's your favorite."

I allow him to lead me inside where I'm greeted by the delectable smell of the meal he's prepared. I can't remember the last time he's cooked for us.

He stops in the hallway before we reach the kitchen, catching me off guard. He pulls his phone out and turns it to me, and I can't help but scowl at the familiar contact page for Ellie's number.

"I'm not showing this to upset you," he explains quickly. "I just wanted you to see me delete her number."

As much as I hate to admit it, it does give me a fair bit of satisfaction to witness him block and delete her. There's no trace of emotion on his face as he does it, no indication that he'll miss her or that he regrets cutting her off. As if for good measure, he navigates into his settings and turns off his password completely, leaving his phone open and unprotected.

"I mean it," he states seriously, his gaze heavy on mine. "You're mine, Julia, and I'm going to start treating you like it."

Those are the exact words I've wanted to hear from him for so long, but now they settle unevenly in my gut, misshapen somehow. I want to be reassured by them, but the doubt slithers through my mind, clouding the sincerity of his declaration.

But I told him I'd give him the chance to show me, and even if he's not a man of his word, I intend to keep mine, and so I muster up a tentative smile.

Satisfied by my expression, Jake takes the risk of holding out his hand toward me. I only hesitate for a moment before I take it and allow him to lead me farther into the house.

I expect him to take me to the kitchen where we eat most of our meals, but instead, he guides me in the opposite direction to the dining room.

A small gasp escapes me as I step across the threshold. He's laid dinner out beautifully, complete with embroidered napkins and our best silverware. Tall white candles burn in sconces, casting flickering shadows through the room. It's like something out of a romance movie, and I can't help the traitorous flutter of my heart as Jake pulls a chair out for me before seating himself.

We eat dinner in silence. The food is perfect, but I find it hard to concentrate on the meal when I can feel the constant weight of my husband's gaze on me.

Once we're done, Jake rises without a word and collects our plates before disappearing off into the kitchen. I lean back in my chair and close my eyes. It's nice to have a moment alone.

Two large hands close over my shoulders, and I jerk forward, letting out a startled yelp at the contact.

"I'm sorry." Jake breathes in my ear. He's so close that I can feel the heat of him fanning against my neck as his fingers massage the knots from my tense shoulders. "I didn't mean to startle you."

In spite of my earlier unease, I find myself relaxing into his touch. I can practically taste his desire as his lips brush over my hair and ghost over the soft skin of my neck. Would it really be so bad to give in? To allow him to give me pleasure after so much pain?

The moan I let out as his teeth nip at my skin is the only answer either of us need.

I tip my head to the side to give him more access. At this silent permission, his hands wander lower, brushing my collarbone. He hooks his thumbs on the thin straps of my dress and then, in one sharp motion, he yanks the fabric hard until the material tears. The bodice of the dress, no longer supported by the straps, crumples forward to reveal my bare breasts.

Jake's never done anything like that before, but I can't even be mad about him ruining my new dress, not with his fingers kneading the hardening peaks of my nipples while he presses hot kisses into the curve of my neck.

A groan tumbles from my lips as I squirm beneath his ministrations, but the hard wood of the chair beneath me offers little relief. Realizing what I'm trying to do, a low chuckle escapes my husband.

Once again, the action is so different from what I'm used to. A small blossom of doubt unfurls within me, but it doesn't last long.

Jake's hands skim down my sides until they reach my hips. He lingers there a second, teasing, before his grip tightens and he forces me forward off the chair.

I cry out in surprise as my breasts push into the cool surface of the table. One of Jake's hands is splayed between my shoulder blades, holding me down. I know I shouldn't like this, but just standing in this position flares the heat inside of me and sends pulses of lust surging through my veins.

One of Jake's legs nudges between my own, forcing me open for him. A blush spreads over me as I realize that the short skirt of my dress isn't covering much of anything.

As if he's reading my thoughts, Jake runs one finger teasingly over me with only the thin lace of my thong between us.

"You're so fucking wet," he hisses. His words are punctuated by the sound of a zipper, and I rock my hips in anticipation as I squirm beneath his firm hold.

"Jake!" I gasp as I feel the tip of him against my entrance. He presses in ever so slightly so that I'm pinned between the table and his cock, unable to escape.

"What do you want?" he demands. There's something dark in his tone, but I'm too far gone to care.

"You," I moan. I attempt to back up onto him, but his hand holds me firmly in place.

"What do you want me to do?" he presses, unmoving.

Frustration builds alongside the pleasure. "I want you to fuck me," I beg.

When he speaks again, I can hear the cold smile in his voice. "And who do you belong to?"

"You," I breathe.

"Me," he confirms. "You're mine."

As a reward, he slams into me, driving me forward against the hard edge of the table. I cry out in equal measure of pain and ecstasy.

The sound seems to spur him on. He pulls out almost all the way before thrusting back into my dripping cunt. It doesn't take him long to set a grueling pace. I can't keep up with him. My legs are buckling beneath me, my body supported only by the table and the cruel pace of his hips.

Sparks of pleasure coalesce as Jake pounds into me. They brighten in intensity until they explode outward with the force of a small star. I cry out, spasming around his cock.

Jake's not far behind. My orgasm sends him over the peak, and he bites down hard on the soft skin of my neck as he spills himself inside of me with an animal groan.

It isn't until later, when he's snoring in bed and I'm freshening up in the bathroom, that I realize he's left a mark. All of my fears flood back as I stare at the semi-circular bruise. Is this really what I want?

Conflicted, I pad back into the bedroom. Jake's sound asleep, but my thoughts are racing too fast for me to consider joining him in bed. Instead, I wander to the window and squint out into the dark night.

My heart stutters as my eyes land on the shadowy clearing in the middle of the swamp. All the graves are gone now, and it should be flat, empty land. But there's something there now, something tall, something shaped rather like a person.

"Jake!" I hiss, not taking my eyes off the thing. When he doesn't stir, I turn toward him and repeat his name a little louder. "Jake!"

He sits up, blinking slowly in the dark. "What?" he slurs.

"There's somebody out in the swamp," I whisper.

Jake shakes his head dismissively. "It's only Amos," he sighs before falling back into bed, snoring once again.

"Seriously, Jake!" I press, but it's no use. He's fast asleep.

Rolling my eyes, I turn back to the window, wanting to get another look at this thing.

But when I focus back on the clearing, the figure is gone.

Only the swamp stares back.

15

DREAM A LITTLE DREAM OF ME

Zeke

The sun hasn't come up yet.

Part of me fears that it may stay night forever.

I sigh and lean against the railing as my eyes scan over the still expanse of the swamp. Although silence hangs in the early morning air, I sense that we're not alone out here on the edge of the shadow-kissed swamp.

"You feel it too?" Miss Penny asks from beside me. I hadn't noticed her materialize, but I'm not particularly surprised. After all, she's not the only ghost who haunts this place.

"Yes, ma'am," I nod, barely taking my eyes off the swaying limbs of the cypress trees. "He's out there."

"Amos is one tough bastard," she huffs. I think that she's being a bit too charitable in her assessment. "Has the sorry excuse for a husband caved?"

A sick feeling blossoms inside of me as I tip my head again. "Almost. I don't know if he can hold Amos back. I don't know if he even *wants* to."

Miss Penny clicks her tongue in a disapproving noise. "What are you going to do?"

"I don't know." I sigh. It's the truth, but it's not good enough. Even though the selfish side of me longs for Julia to stay in Hahnville, I understand that her leaving will keep her safe. Amos is persistent, but he's also weaker than he's ever been. I doubt he'll be able to follow her all the way to New York.

But she hasn't left.

Amos made sure of that.

I try not to dwell on the sounds I'd heard emanating from the house last night. It had been so hard to linger at the edge of the swamp through those moans, but I hadn't wanted to leave Julia entirely alone, not with Amos.

The image of them together in my mind has me seeing red.

"Calm down, son," Miss Penny advises. Her tone is practical, but there's an edge of sympathy there too. "There's still time."

"Amos won't let her leave," I counter. "What am I supposed to do?"

"Tell her the truth?" the shade of the old woman suggests.

It's a preposterous idea. The second I go to Julia raving like a madman about demons in the swamp, she'll write me off entirely. Even though she's seen things she clearly can't explain, I don't know if she's ready for all of the grisly details.

As if picking up on my thoughts, Miss Penny adds, "The *whole* truth."

"You know I can't do that," I huff.

"Well, you've got to do something or else we'll lose her. And if Amos takes Julia, who knows what that will do to his power, especially now that his attachment to the Gregory line has been severed."

She's right. I've got to do something.

My mind made up, I turn toward the house and squint up at the bedroom window. It's still dark, and I imagine that the occupants are still asleep.

"Good luck," Miss Penny intones.

I don't have time to reply before she fades away into the gray swirl of the dawn.

Left with no choice, I silently slip inside the house and away from Amos's prying eyes.

Everything feels muted at this early hour. The hallway is shrouded in darkness, and the only noise comes from the hum of the air conditioning as it struggles against the cloying heat of the marsh. I creep up the stairs, my feet making no sound as I reach the landing and survey the second floor.

I find the master bedroom easily, but I pause before opening the door.

Invading Julia's privacy like this is wrong. But she's in more danger than she knows, and if this is the only way I can save her, then I have no choice.

Steeling myself, I step into the bedroom.

I notice Jake first. He's lying on the side of the bed closest to the door, his form crumpled beneath a mass of blankets. By the sound of his snores, it would take a blast from a small nuclear bomb to rouse him.

Julia, however, is partially awake.

Her eyes, heavy with sleep, find mine in the semi-darkness. I brace myself for her to scream at my sudden intrusion, but instead, a soft, exhausted smile spreads across her face.

"Zeke?" she whispers, her voice threaded with slumber.

"It's me," I confirm. I cross quietly to her and kneel beside the bed so that our faces are level. We can talk more quietly this way, and hopefully we won't wake up Jake.

Her smile widens, and something within me flutters as my gaze fixes on the delicate curve of her mouth. I can't help but remember how her lips felt on mine, or the heat of her body against mine as we kissed.

Julia reaches out a tentative hand, her fingers ghosting over my cheek. "What are you doing here, Zeke?" she asks, her voice husky and low.

"I...." My voice trails off as her manicured nails gently trace the line of my mouth. What am I supposed to tell her? That she's in danger from a demon that haunts the swamp? That her husband is slowly, but surely, crumbling beneath the weight of hell's promise? That I think she's the most beautiful woman I've ever seen?

It turns out that I don't need to say anything at all.

Before I can stop her, Julia leans forward and presses her lips gently against my own. It's a sweet kiss, full of hope. Who am I to deny her that?

Her hand weaves into my hair, her fingers massaging into my scalp. I want to touch her. I *need* to touch her. But it's taking all of my energy just to focus on the joining of our lips.

Sensing my hesitation, Julia pulls back and regards me almost sadly. "I wish you visited me in more than just my dreams," she confesses.

Her dreams?

A thrill runs through me as I realize what she means. How many times have I visited her in the dark hours of the night? Has she imagined my mouth on her, my hands teasing and my hips against hers? Just the thought of it makes my cock start to stiffen, pushing uncomfortably against the confines of my trousers.

And she thinks *this* is a dream too, I realize. And in a dream, anything is possible.

A wicked thought overtakes me as my eyes slide over to Jake. If Amos could do it, why can't I?

It's a strange but quick process, but once it's complete, I'm like a new man.

I roll over, and Julia starts at the sudden movement beside her.

"Jake?" she asks, though her tone is gilded with doubt. When I don't answer, she asks in a smaller, more astonished, voice, "Zeke?"

I grin lazily at her.

"How is this possible?" she gasps as she reaches out to cup my face for a second time. The sensation of skin against skin is overwhelming, and I melt beneath her touch. In that instant, I know that I want to make her feel just as good.

"It's not." I feel bad about the white lie, but I don't know how else to explain it. "It's just a dream."

Her face crumples into a petulant frown, and I almost laugh at how comically disappointed she looks.

"If this is just a dream, then it won't matter if I do this," Julia whispers before closing the distance between us.

The sweet slide of her lips against mine is dizzying. I can't remember the last time I'd felt so *alive.* Finally able to touch her, I reach out and pull her close, taking the opportunity to run my hands over the smooth curves of her body. To my delight, I realize that she's mostly naked under the blanket, with only a thin pair of panties to protect her modesty.

One of my hands drifts upward to find the soft peak of her breast, and she mewls against my mouth as I roll her nipple between my fingers. Her hips jerk against mine, grinding against my hardening length.

Without breaking the kiss, I kick off my pants, freeing myself from the confines of the fabric. My cock brushes against Julia's belly, and we both groan at the sensation.

If this is the only night I get with Julia, I want her to know how much she means to me. I want her to understand how amazing she is, how she deserves to be cherished.

I pull back from her lips and trail a path of hot kisses down the sleek column of her neck. I pause for a moment to nip at one of her breasts before continuing my journey south.

When I finally reach my destination, my breath hitches in my throat as I realize how wet she is. She's soaked through her thong, and now I can't wait to taste her. She lifts her hips to allow me to slide her panties down her legs, and then I dive in.

The sounds I coax from her lips are like heaven. I work my tongue against her slick heat, savoring the way her thighs clamp around me as her hips buck wildly in pleasure. The taste of her is exquisite. I drink from her eagerly, sending her careening toward the edge of ecstasy.

Her mouth opens in a small, silent gasp as she comes hard on my face, but I give her no time to rest.

Nearly undone from the anticipation alone, I move back up to capture her lips in a searing kiss. At the same time, I finally wrap a hand around my cock and guide myself to her core. I sigh heavily as I run my length against her slick folds, relishing the feel of her.

Julia moans with need beneath me, shifting her hips in an effort to increase the friction.

"Patience, sweetheart," I caution with a chuckle, and she pouts again. I decide that this is my favorite expression on her, and I wish that there were some way I could enjoy this side of her every single day.

But I'm not the kind of man to keep a lady waiting, so I dutifully position myself at her entrance before sliding inside in one smooth, torturous stroke.

Julia shudders, lost in the sensation. It's all I can do not to lose it right then and there. I take a few deep breaths as she adjusts around me. Her skin is like silk against mine, squeezing me in all the right places.

Finally, when I get myself under control again, I pull out slowly. The way her inner walls massage my cock is almost blinding in intensity, but I try to stifle the sensation so I don't disappoint her. I focus instead on pushing back in, relishing the wanton moans that spill out from her delicate lips as I spear her, again and again, on my length.

I know I'm not going to last as long as she deserves, so I decide to speed up the process. I reach down between us with one hand and find the hooded bud of her clit. When she cries out at my ministrations, I swallow them up with a kiss.

Her muscles flutter around me, and I know she's close. It only takes a few more powerful strokes for her to tumble over the edge. She clenches around me, ushering in my own orgasm as her pussy greedily claims the full length of my cock.

Lights explode behind my eyes, and I collapse on top of her, my chest heaving against her breasts as I struggle to come down. Not wanting to crush her, I roll to the side, though I keep my arms wrapped around her in a protective embrace.

It's almost light out now. In the tenuous glow of the dawn, Julia stares up at me through half-lidded eyes. A satisfied smile stretches across her face, and in that moment, it's my dearest wish to be able to lie here with her every day.

The desire wells within me so ferociously that I'm unable to stop myself from blurting out, "I love you."

Julia's mouth parts in surprise, and I immediately want to disappear. How could I have said something so stupid?

"Who are you?" Julia whispers. Her eyes search mine as though the answers are hidden there instead of in our hearts. "Are you Jake? Or Zeke?"

Blood roars through my ears. "Which do you want me to be?" I ask softly, knowing that my very being might come crashing down with her answer.

A tear wells in the corner of her eye. "I don't know," she replies, clearly torn. "Is this even real?"

I reach up and brush the tear away.

"It's only a dream," I assure her. "It's only a dream."

16

RAMBLINGS OF A MADWOMAN

Julia

To say I'm royally confused when I wake up is an understatement.

I sit up groggily, blinking back sleep. My thoughts are a jumbled mess, and my body still rings from the ghost of this morning's encounter. Logically, I know it was a dream. So why did it feel so real?

An image of Zeke kneeling beside the bed flashes through my mind, and I can't help but blush at the intensity that flared in his honeyed eyes. But he couldn't have been here. That's just silly.

"It was just a dream," I murmur into the empty bedroom, as if the words could convince my harried thoughts.

"What was that?" Jake's voice calls from the ensuite bathroom. It takes me a moment to register the sound of the shower, and then realization hits me like a brick.

Jake and I fucked last night.

And we'd made love this morning, hadn't we?

It still seemed so hazy. I could have sworn it had been Zeke's face

113

hovering over me as he moved so reverently inside of me. Things with Jake had never been like that. They were either drearily boring, or crazy like last night. I must have been so tired that I dreamed it, or maybe I was just half asleep for round two.

I want to groan out loud at how Jake had pounded me into the table yesterday. How had I given in so easily? I don't even know if I can forgive him yet, but he's already back in my bed after one nice dinner.

What does that say about me?

I don't even want to think about it. Luckily, Jake provides a distraction by turning off the shower and stepping out into the bedroom, dripping and covered only by a towel slung low over his hips.

He grins at me, but it's nothing like the lazy smile he'd flashed at me this morning.

"Sleep well?" he asks cockily. His eyes drift down from mine, and I blush when I realize that when I'd sat up earlier, the covers had pooled around my middle, exposing my bare breasts to the morning sunlight.

"Other than that one interruption," I say, trying to mimic his confidence.

"What interruption?" he asks. He looks genuinely confused.

So maybe it really *was* a dream.

I don't want to dwell on what it means that I dreamt of making sweet love to Zeke instead of my husband, and so I wave it away.

"Never mind," I dismiss.

Jake shrugs but doesn't question it. "I hate to say it, baby, but I've got to go into the office today." He pauses, as though he expects me to protest, but I'm secretly glad to have some space and time to think. "I've already turned on my location on my phone so you don't have to worry about where I am." He says it sheepishly. The insidious, doubtful side of me whispers that it seems too rehearsed to be genuine.

"Okay," I reply after an awkward pause.

He lingers for a moment before he moves again. I get the sense that he's not sure what to make of my short answers. Eventually, he shrugs for a second time and then heads to the walk-in closet.

I watch with idle curiosity as he dresses in a fresh suit, gathers the rest of his things, and then swoops in for a quick kiss. It's a little too forceful, but I return it dutifully.

"I'll be back tonight," he assures me, and then he's gone. A moment later, the front door slams, followed shortly by the crunch of gravel as he drives away.

I sit in bed for a few more minutes, contemplating the day that stretches ahead of me. I hate being alone in this house, but I don't exactly have anybody to call. There's no point in going shopping again. I can't even distract myself by talking to the workers out in the swamp now that they've finishing moving the graves and are waiting on the final permits to start draining the marsh

Still, I can't just languish here like some distressed Victorian woman. Instead, I decide to start with my normal morning routine and just go from there.

I take my time in the shower, washing all signs of sex from my body. My muscles are sore, and my hair is tangled, but I do the best I can. After that, I gather up one of my favorite dresses, a matching pair of heels, and a set of lingerie. I slide into my clothes and am just about to start on my makeup when I hear a car pull into the driveway.

Who could it be?

It's not like I have any friends who would just come popping over on a whim. Maybe Jake decided to stay home after all?

I hurry to the window and peek out through the blinds, catching a glimpse of a familiar car.

Of course, it's Helen, our closest neighbor. Even though only a few weeks have passed since she last stopped by, it feels like it's been an eternity. While I normally don't appreciate unannounced guests, I find myself relieved by her sudden presence.

I'm already downstairs and throwing the front door open before she's even made it to the front stoop.

"Good morning, Julia," she greets me, her southern manners outweighing her surprise at my appearance.

"Hello, Helen," I reply. I'm unable to keep the relief out of my voice, and she picks up on it immediately.

The older woman's eyes narrow. "Is everything okay, honey?"

There's something about the warm way she says it that reminds me of my late mom. Tears shimmer in my eyes and cloud my vision as I shake my head.

Helen's gaze lands on my eye, and I realize with burgeoning horror that I haven't put on my makeup yet, and by extension, I haven't plastered foundation over the ugly bruise that Jake's hand left on my cheekbone.

"Oh, honey," Helen sighs, and the pity in her voice shatters something inside of me.

The tears finally come out in choking sobs as I bury my face in my hands. Shame hits me first, followed hard by a punch of fear.

What must Helen think of me? She probably thinks I'm some weak, pathetic trophy wife who lets herself be tossed around by her bullish husband. Is that really what I've become? When did I lose so much of myself? How did I even get here?

Helen's arms wrap around me and pull me into a matronly hug. She soothes me as I cry, stroking my hair like I'm a child and cooing calming platitudes into my ear. It's exactly what I need, and that only breaks me down more.

Finally, I compose myself enough to pull away. I don't look at the older woman. I'm afraid to see the judgment in her eyes.

But she clasps her hands on my shoulders, forcing me to meet her gaze. All I find there is a spark of fierce protection, the sign of a woman who's seen more of life than I have and has vowed to never let bad things happen to anybody else.

"Your husband did this?" It's clear by the way she asks that she already knows the answer.

I nod, since there's no point in hiding it.

"What do you want to do about it?"

"I don't know," I force out.

"Whatever you need, I'll help you," Helen assures me. "You

wouldn't be the first young lady in Hahnville who's needed to get away from a violent man."

"He… Jake's not violent," I protest. I don't know why I feel the need to defend him after what he did. "This is the only time he's ever done anything like this."

Helen shakes her head. "The first time, you mean." Her eyes harden as though she's just made an important decision. "How much do you know about the history of this land?" she asks.

The question is a curveball, and I find myself answering automatically with the little information I've got. "There used to be a huge old house here, but it burned down. That's why Jake was able to buy the land at such a good price."

"That house has stood on the edge of this swamp for generations," Helen says. "The Gregory family lived here up until Miss Penny's niece sold the plot to you. If she'd known that it was still here, she never would have done it."

"What's still here?"

Helen's eyes shift toward the swamp, and I'm overcome by the intense surety that something is watching us from the trees.

When she speaks again, her voice is hushed and tinged with fear. "This is an unholy place, Julia. Somewhere down the Gregory line, one of the ancestors called something forth from the swamp. Since then, it's murdered countless people, practically everybody who was unfortunate enough to step foot on this land. It gets inside their heads, the men in particular, and makes them do terrible things. But it loves the women especially."

I don't want to believe what she's saying. It sounds like the ramblings of a madwoman. And yet, every part of me is screaming that it's all true.

"It wanted Layla, Miss Penny's niece. They burned the house down to try to get rid of it. Then it went after Bailey, the contractor's girl. When she got away, I was sure she'd put an end to it, but I just can't shake the feeling that it's back."

The fear is plain on Helen's face. I think about all the times I've felt sure that somebody was standing just behind me but turned around to find nothing. I've seen figures out in the swamp. Then there was that weird incident with Tanner, who wasn't even supposed to be in the state.

"I've heard things," I admit after a long moment.

She nods, encouraging me.

"I've… experienced things. Things that I can't explain."

"You've seen it," Helen states. It's not a question, not when she already knows the truth that I'm so hesitant to share.

I don't want to believe it, but I know she's right.

I know that something is out there.

I draw in a deep breath. I'm aware that to say the words, to admit them out loud, would be giving in to the impossible.

Finally, I steel myself as demand, "What is it? What's out there?"

Helen regards me for a moment, assessing how serious I am. I hold her gaze steadily, determined to show her that I'm ready to know the truth.

"A demon," she says. "Asmodeus."

My mind flashes back to the figure I'd seen last night out in the abandoned cemetery in the swamp. Who had Jake said it was?

"Amos," I murmur.

Helen's eyes widen in shock.

Somewhere out in the distant marsh, the sound of singing floats on the wind.

Folks, I'm goin' down to St. James infirmary…

17

BOUND TO THIS PLACE

Zeke

"I'm a terrible person."

I'm back on the porch with Miss Penny, who's regarding me with an unreadable expression. I have no doubt that she knows what happened this morning, the same way she's aware of everything that goes on in this house.

I don't need her to tell me that I fucked up. I was supposed to warn Julia about the threat Amos poses, not claim her. Even though she'd thought it was a dream, I still had no right to trick her like that. I feel so guilty that I can hardly think about anything else.

"Do you regret it?" Miss Penny asks suddenly, breaking me from my cocoon of self-pity.

I shake my head. "It was amazing," I admit abashedly. "But I feel like I took advantage of her. How can I ever fix this?"

"You start by doing right by her," she replies sternly. "You need to come clean."

I hate that she's right. It would be far easier to just pretend it never happened, but I owe Julia so much more than that. She deserves to be treated with honesty and respect.

She deserves the truth.

Miss Penny wanders off a short while later, leaving me to contemplate my next move as I stare blankly out at the swamp. There's nothing much for me to do but ruminate until I hear Helen's car retreating down the driveway.

It's now or never.

Not giving myself a chance to reconsider, I abandon my post on the porch and step inside the house, making a beeline for the kitchen.

Julia sits on a stool at the island, scrolling through her cell phone.

"Zeke!" she exclaims, dropping the device in surprise. It lands on the granite countertop with a dull thud. She presses one hand to her heart and shakes her head. "You scared me!"

"I'm sorry," I apologize quickly. I've barely said a few words, and I'm already fucking this up even more. "I didn't mean to barge in like this. The back door was open and I–"

Julia holds up one hand, cutting me off. "Don't worry about it," she dismisses. "I need to ask you something. Do you believe in curses?"

Shocked, I linger in the doorway. I'd expected her to be upset with me about simply walking into her house, but she doesn't seem concerned with that at all. Instead, she's strangely excited.

"What's happened?" I ask, hoping that Amos hasn't gotten to her and that I'm not too late.

"There's something out in the swamp," she says. Her eyes search mine in the seconds that follow, desperately looking for any sign of ridicule.

"I know," I reply simply. "That's what I came to tell you."

It's Julia's turn to be stunned. "I don't mean, like, an animal," she says slowly, as though she thinks I've misunderstood. "It's... something else."

Relief surges through me as I realize that she knows. Helen was here earlier, wasn't she? I bet she's the one who told Julia.

"I know it sounds crazy," Julia rambles when I don't respond. "But I've seen things there in the marsh. A man that's not a man. And I've heard things. There were footsteps upstairs and children laughing. And then Tanner showed up, but I don't think it was actually him. I think it just *looked* like him..."

"How much did Helen tell you?" I ask, interrupting her stream of consciousness. "About this land? About the swamp?"

Julia eyes me anxiously. I can tell she doesn't know whether I believe her or not. Finally, she says, "I know about the murders, if that's what you mean."

I nod. "What else?"

"People see things out here. Helen told me about... an entity."

"A demon," I state. She flinches as the word.

"So you believe it?" she gasps, finally understanding that I'm serious. "You don't think I'm crazy?"

I want to laugh at the sheer absurdity of the situation, but I don't want Julia to think I'm making fun of her, so I bite it back. Instead, I answer, "No, you're not crazy. Amos is real."

Julia's gaze shoots to mine at the mention of the demon's name. "You've seen it?" she presses.

"I have," I admit. "That's part of what I wanted to talk to you about. I've had the deep misfortune of knowing Amos personally."

A shocked gasp escapes from Julia's lips. "What happened? Did it hurt you?" She stands up and reaches for me, clasping my hands in hers as she looks me over in concern.

I shake my head. "Don't worry about me," I assure her. Someday I'll tell her about my run in with Amos, but not today. "You're the one who's in danger."

Fear flashes across Julia's delicate features, but she doesn't seem surprised. Helen must have already told her what Amos wants. "I know," she confirms softly. In spite of the terror, her eyes shine with hard determination. "I'm not going to let it hurt me. Helen and I have a plan."

"A plan?" I repeat. It's going to have to be one hell of a strategy if they're hoping to take down a demon.

"We're going down to New Orleans later this afternoon. Helen knows somebody she thinks can help."

It's a pretty thought, but not a practical one. "Amos is strong," I caution. "He won't go down without a fight." I know that firsthand, and I can't help but think that it's a losing battle, no matter what kind of power they've got on their side.

"I have to try," Julia insists. "What else am I supposed to do?"

I squeeze her hands in mine. "You could run," I urge. "Get out of here and run as far away from this godforsaken swamp as you can get."

"I can't," she claims, but I hear the doubt in her voice.

"You *can*," I argue. "Leave while you still have time."

"And what about you?"

I blink, not understanding. "What do you mean?"

"I'm not going to leave you here in Hahnville with an actual demon running loose," she scoffs, rolling her eyes. Then something bright passes over her expression and she adds, "Come with me."

The suggestion is staggering. Does she understand what she's saying? One look at her tells me that she does, and that she's dead serious.

"I can't," I whisper in a voice broken with regret. God, I want to. I'd give anything to go with her, to follow her anywhere she wants to wander. The thought of it makes my heart ache.

"Please," she begs, squeezing my hands in her own. I recall all of the places my fingers touched this morning, and I think I'd cry if I could.

"I want to," I manage to force out. "I really fucking want to."

"So do it." She says it as though it's the simplest thing in the world.

But it's not. How can I explain what ties me here? How can I face the betrayal and fear in her eyes once she knows who I really am?

"You can't tell me you didn't feel it when we kissed," she presses, her hands releasing mine to run over my chest. "That spark was like nothing I've ever felt before."

A lump catches in my throat, and I feel sick to my stomach because she's right. There is something special between us. Maybe that's why I'm here, why I was drawn to the old Gregory property in the first place. Maybe Julia and I were always meant to meet.

But why did it have to be like this?

Julia's fingers curl into the fabric of my shirt. She's so close that our chests are almost touching. If I lean down just a few inches, my lips will be on hers, and we'll be able to lose ourselves in one another.

"I want you," I confess. "More than anything. More than life itself."

"Then take me," Julia challenges. Heat simmers behind her eyes, a wildfire of desire barely held at bay.

I want to give in. Oh God, I fucking want her. I can feel my resolve crumbling with each passing second as the flames of her desire lick over me.

But I can't.

I *can't.*

"You dream about me," I breathe. I'm unable to look away from the goddess that burns before me.

Biting her lip, she nods.

"Tell me what you dream about."

Her mouth quirks up in a coquettish smirk. "I dream about your hands on me," she starts as she takes one last step toward me, closing the distance between us. She leans in, and her next words fan tantalizingly over the shell of my ear. "And your tongue."

This is a terrible idea, but I can't seem to bring myself to stop her as her hands trace down my chest toward the riveted planes of my abs. My cock stiffens in anticipation, and I know she must feel my hardening length pressing against her belly.

I allow myself the pleasure of feeling her fingers toy with the button of my trousers before I grab her hands in mine, stopping her progress.

"I want this," I say earnestly, hoping she understands just how serious I am. "I want you. But I can't."

Hurt flashes in Julia's eyes, and she takes a step back. The molten heat between us recedes by a few degrees, but it's still there, raging in the negative space between us.

"Is it because of Jake?" she asks in a defeated tone.

I shake my head vehemently.

"Then what?" she demands.

"It's complicated," I sigh. "I can't leave Hahnville."

Julia tips her face down toward the floor, and I realize she doesn't want me to see the tears that well in her eyes. "Fine," she sniffles. "I understand."

"You don't," I insist. "I want to go with you. I want us to be together. But we can't. We're too… different."

"I see," she replies sardonically. I realize too late what she thinks I mean.

I open my mouth to finally tell her the truth like she deserves, but I'm not even able to get a single word out before the sound of a car in the driveway interrupts.

"That must be Helen," Julia mutters. "I need to leave."

"Julia, wait," I implore, but she's already pushing past me into the hallway.

My heart breaks as I watch her retreat. She only pauses at the front door. Without turning around she says, "Goodbye, Zeke."

And then she's gone, the door slamming behind her in her wake.

I stand there until the shadows lengthen, unwilling to accept defeat. It isn't until evening falls that I feel Miss Penny's presence at my elbow.

"You did your best," she consoles.

"No, I didn't. I just made it worse."

Miss Penny shakes her head. "You tried, and that's what counts."

How can that be true when the only thing that counts to me just walked out that door with one final goodbye?

I've lost her.

I failed.

I have nothing else to exist for.

18

GHOST OF A CHANCE

Julia

"Are you sure about this?"

Helen flashes me a reassuring smile. "This isn't the first time I've gone to see Mama Janvier," she says.

It's not lost on me that my neighbor looks like the last person who'd put any stock into the craft of a Voodoo priestess, but who am I to judge? Helen had promised her friend would know what to do, and it's not like I have any other options.

I peer out the passenger side window of the car as Helen pulls into the driveway of an old stately home. We're in the suburbs of New Orleans, a part I've never been before. The houses here are larger and look like they had probably been grand once, but years of harsh weather and lack of upkeep have caught up with many of the buildings.

I think about my new house on the edge of the swamp and shudder. Is this what our home will look like soon after years of exposure and neglect?

We climb out of the vehicle and into the summer heat. The humidity is a little more bearable now that we've put some distance between us and the marsh, but it's warmer here. By the time we reach the screened in porch, my dress is already sticking to the small of my back.

Helen doesn't bother to knock. She simply pulls the porch door open like she's been here a thousand times and ushers me across the porch to the interior door.. Even though she told me she called ahead, I still feel awkward about it.

At the door to the house, Helen presses the doorbell. A wheezy chime sounds inside, shortly followed by a set of shuffling footsteps within.

The door swings open to reveal a statuesque woman who, even in a pair of flat shoes, towers over me. Her skin is the color of coffee, and her ivory hair frizzes out from under a purple headscarf. Dark, ancient eyes peer down at me from a face etched deeply with smile lines.

"Helen," the woman says in greeting, reaching out for my neighbor and catching her in a warm embrace.

"Thank you for seeing us on such short notice," Helen says after pressing a kiss to the woman's cheek.

"No need to thank me," she smiles. Then she turns to me and pulls me in for an equally familiar hug. "You must be Julia!"

"It's nice to meet you, Miss Janvier," I reply politely. I'm not used to this level of affection, especially from a person I've just met.

The Voodoo priestess waves one bangled arm in the air, as if dismissing my formality. "Call me Mama Janvier," she says. "Everybody else does. Now won't you two come inside?"

I follow Helen and Mama Janvier into the bungalow with some trepidation. My only knowledge of Voodoo comes from questionable depictions in movies, so I have no idea what to expect.

The interior of the house is relatively normal. Mama Janvier brings us to the living room where Helen and I sink down onto a comfortable, overstuffed chintz couch. There's a sweating pitcher of iced tea and three glasses already set out on the coffee table, a reminder that Helen had arranged this visit in advance.

After pouring each a glass of us tea, Mama Janvier settles into an armchair opposite us and regards me with an assessing stare. I'm not sure what she's looking for, but she seems to find it and offers me a satisfied nod.

"You've got demon troubles," she states.

I shoot a questioning glance over at Helen, silently asking if she'd shared the nature of my problems when she'd called earlier, but my neighbor simply shakes her head.

Unsettled, I ask, "How did you know?"

"Its influence is all over you," Mama Janvier replies, as though it's the most obvious thing in the world. "Asmodeus. And you're not the first one to try to rid that swamp of the evil that walks there."

My eyes once again shift over to Helen, who shrugs. "Mama Janvier was my nanny, way back in the day. She raised me out there, and she always made sure I knew how to protect myself," she explains.

"I had my work cut out for me," Mama Janvier confirms. "Asmodeus is one nasty piece of work."

"If you've dealt with Amos before, then how come it's still around?" I ask.

The Voodoo priestess sighs. "The circumstances have changed. The demon has always walked that land, but for centuries, it was bound only to the Gregory line. The spell I'd given Helen before was meant to suppress Asmodeus as long as it remained tied to the family."

"So it's no longer bound?" I question. "How did that happen?"

"In order to bind this demon, its true name must be carved into a cemetery stone and sealed away. As long as that seal remains intact, the bond cannot be severed."

"So something broke the seal?" Helen interjects.

I think back to something the workmen told me about finding a weird rock in an old box. Didn't they say there was a word etched into it—a name?

The sickened look on my face must give me away because Mama Janvier's gaze falls on me, so I explain to her what the crew found.

"They let it out," Helen murmurs when I'm done. "That's why the spell couldn't hold it any longer."

"And a spell won't be enough this time," the Voodoo priestess adds. "The demon is still tied to the land, but its will is now its own. Its hunger will be strong, even if its powers have been weakened."

"What do we do?" I understand that leaving won't solve the problem. It'll just pass on to whoever ends up in that house next. No, it has to stop here–with me.

Sensing my determination, Mama Janvier smiles. "The incantation will suppress it, but you have to bind it to a living soul first. The sacrifice of that soul is the only way to banish the demon for good."

Fear tremors through me as I realize what she means. Somebody is going to have to die if we want to get rid of Amos for good. It's too much to ask, too much to even contemplate.

As Helen and I sit in shocked silence, Mama Janvier produces a small, oddly shaped bottle seemingly from thin air and presses it into my shaking hand.

"The sacrificial soul must drink this before the incantation is spoken, and it must happen in the swamp where the demon resides," she says.

"I… I can't," I stammer as I try to push the potion back at her, but she won't take it from me.

"Keep it," she insists. "You may change your mind."

I won't.

I can't.

And yet, I find myself slipping the vial into my purse, out of sight, and hopefully, out of mind. Even though I don't believe in the power of Voodoo, the thought of using this potion on another person sickens me.

Desperately wanting to change the subject from human sacrifice to literally anything else, I ask, "What about the ghosts?"

The voodoo priestess nods thoughtfully. "Those are the spirits of the souls buried in the cemetery in the swamp and those that have died in the house. When the workmen disturbed their graves, the spirits were broken from their rest."

"The children," I realize, thinking of the sounds of laughter that sometimes drifted down from the upper floors.

"And they aren't the only ones," Mama Janvier adds.

"Are they dangerous?" Helen inquires, clearly concerned for my safety.

"Quite the opposite," Mama Janvier replies. "Many of them were victims of the demon, and now they work to protect others from its influence. It may very well be why Julia has yet to succumb to Asmodeus's dark designs."

I don't like the way she says that, as if it's only a matter of time before I fall prey to the demon's clutches. Between that and the small bottle of dubious liquid hiding away in my purse, I decide that we're done here.

"Thank you, Mama Janvier." I stand up quickly, bumping my shins against the coffee table and causing the ice to rattle in the untouched glasses of tea. "But it's getting late, and I think we'd better be going."

Helen raises a questioning eyebrow but seems to pick up on my discomfort. "Julia's right," she agrees. "We really should head back before the traffic gets bad."

We say our goodbyes, and I endure another stifling hug before we're able to escape. Neither of us speaks until we're in the car and pulling out of the driveway.

"What do you think?" Helen asks hesitantly as she navigates the narrow streets of the neighborhood.

"Helen, I don't mean to insult you at all, but I'm pretty sure that woman just told me to murder somebody," I blurt out.

"Everything comes at a price," she replies softly. "It's up to each of us to decide whether it's worth paying."

Those words run through my mind as we head back to Hahnville. By the time we reach Helen's house, where she's promised to give me the incantation, I still haven't worked out exactly what she means.

An older man steps out onto the porch to greet us as we pull up at the side of Helen's house. He walks with a cane and limps slightly, but his lack of mobility doesn't seem to have a negative impact on his mood. He's got a kind face and, like Helen, I decide that I immediately like him.

"You must be Miss Julia," he says as I step onto the porch. He shakes my hand with a firm grip. "I'm Robert. It's good to meet you."

"Likewise," I smile, and I truly mean it.

"Come on in," he urges, ushering Helen and I inside. "I've put some coffee on for you girls." As his wife passes, I notice him plant a tender kiss on her temple, and she shoots him a loving glance in return. It's such an intimate moment that I feel almost like an intruder seeing it.

As we settle into the kitchen with our coffee, I try to imagine Jake and I growing old like that, but I simply can't picture it. The realization weighs heavily on me, and it's with a troubled heart that I absently nod yes to Robert's offer to show me his research, whatever that means.

It's not until he reappears several minutes later carrying a cardboard banker's box overflowing with photographs and newspaper clippings that I understand exactly what his research entails.

"This is everything I've got on the demon," he proclaims proudly as he sets the box on the kitchen table in front of me.

"So you believe it too?" I ask. I don't know why I'm so surprised given Helen's certainty.

"Not until recently," Robert admits as he eases into a chair across from Helen and me. "I'd thought it was all just local legend until last year when I saw it for myself."

"You saw Amos?" I gasp.

"Up close and personal," he confirms. He gestures down to his leg and then the cane he uses for support. "I can't say that it was a pleasant meeting. After it happened, I decided to find out everything I could about the demon. As it turns out, there's a lot of information out there, if you know where to look."

He shuffles around through the box for a moment before extracting a yellowed newspaper. He reads the bold print of the headline out loud, stating, "Police seek suspect in swamp serial killing. That's from 1967, by the way."

He sets the paper down and selects a thick manila folder from the box. There's a stamp on the front boasting the insignia of the local parish police department. "This is a copy of the police reports from the old Gregory place," he explains. He flips the folder open and spreads out the documents, but I barely take any notice of them.

Instead, a photograph sticking out of the box hooks my gaze. The picture is in black and white, but it's so old that the fraying edges are splotchy and yellow. But even with the discoloration, the eyes that gaze blankly back at me are far too familiar.

Noticing my preoccupation, Robert takes the opportunity to pull the photograph free and place it in front of me. "Ah, this is an interesting one," he says. "These three men were doing some construction at the old Gregory place back in the 1930s. This photo was taken just hours before one of the workmen was killed in a terrible accident. Of course, we know now that Amos probably had a hand in it. They ended up burying the man in the cemetery in the swamp, if I remember correctly. Sad business."

I can't tear my eyes from the central figure in the photograph. "Which one died?" I ask in a quivering voice.

Even before Robert points to the smiling young man in the middle, I already know the answer. His confirmation is just the final nail in the coffin.

"Julia, are you okay?" Helen asks, finally picking up on my growing horror.

I don't answer. Instead, I turn back to Robert. "What was his name?" I demand. "The man who died?"

Robert and Helen exchange an uneasy glance before he replies, "Hezekiah James. He died in 1931."

Blood turns to ice in my veins. I recall the gravestone that the workmen had carried to the truck, the one bearing the same name as the man standing in the photo before me, the man with eyes the color of honey that still shine with kindness even after a hundred years.

"Zeke," I breathe, hardly able to utter the title out loud. "His name is Zeke."

And with that realization, the world shatters around me.

Zeke is dead.

The man I'm falling for is a ghost.

19

TELLING HER THE TRUTH

Zeke

I can't bring myself to leave.

Even after Miss Penny's attempt to comfort me, I can't seem to find the strength in me to let Julia go. No matter how final her goodbye was, I just can't abandon her, not when Amos's sights are still set so squarely upon her.

I linger in the hallway until the shadows blossom out into darkness. Nobody living has ventured inside for hours, and with a heavy heart, I start to wonder if Julia really has taken my advice and fled.

My aggrieved thoughts drive me toward the living room where I turn on the lights in order to study the photographs of Julia and Jake that line the decorative mantelpiece. She looks happy in some of the earlier ones, but that spark of joy seems to fade in each picture as I move chronologically past the frames.

How I wish I could give her more than this life she's built with Jake. The cruelty of fate isn't lost on me as I wonder why we've been brought together now, only for us to never truly be together.

133

I don't know how much time passes before the crunch of gravel in the driveway alerts me that somebody has come home.

A mix of relief and trepidation claw through me as I hear the familiar tones of Julia's voice, followed by the clack of her heels against the gravel as she approaches the front door.

The air changes as soon as Julia steps inside the house. I want to see her, but I fear that she'll hate me even more if she knows I'm here. Still, the longing is too great, so I allow myself to fade into nothing just as she walks into the living room.

Julia stiffens immediately, as though she's felt the disturbance of my presence in the air.

"Zeke?" she calls tentatively.

It's my turn to freeze.

Something's different.

Julia isn't simply trying to determine if I'm still in the house. It's like she's aware of my presence here as I keep my silent vigil over her.

I don't understand how, but she *knows*.

There's no point in hiding now. I'm resigned for what's to come, be it fear or rage. I've lied to her and hidden the truth. I can't blame her for being upset with me.

Summoning the power, I take form in front of her, coalescing from the shadows until I appear as solid as the walls around us.

Julia's mouth falls open in a gasp of disbelief. Her wide eyes shine in the soft light. I expect her to scream, but she doesn't.

"It's really true," she whispers in a voice hushed with awe. "You're…"

"Dead," I finish for her.

I can practically hear the gears of her mind turning. One hand reaches for me and comes to rest on my chest, directly over my heart. I know she can feel no beat there, no rhythm of life.

"You're a ghost," she murmurs, her tone filled more with wonder than the disgust I'd so feared. "Why didn't you tell me?"

I bring my hand up, ensconcing her slim fingers in my own. "I wanted to," I promise. "But I didn't know how."

A bolt of anger flashes through her eyes. "You should have told me."

"Would you have believed me if I had?" The words are harsh, but my tone is soft. "How did you figure it out?"

"Helen's husband showed me a photograph. You were in it, but it was taken in 1931 just before you… you died."

She tilts her head down as she steps into me, her cheek coming to rest against the flat plane of my chest. I don't have much energy left, but I've got enough to wrap my arms tightly around her, holding her to me.

"You've been watching over me this whole time," Julia murmurs into the fabric of my shirt. Hot tears seep through the cloth, and I realize that she's crying.

"I've tried to keep you safe," I say as I press a kiss to the top of her head. "Even if you can never trust me again, please believe that I'll do anything in my power to keep Amos from hurting you."

She draws back slightly to stare up at me with those shining green eyes. She searches my face as though she's trying to find any dishonesty there. The fire that burned so brightly within her this morning is back, a single ember that quickly flares in the space between us.

I need her to know that I'm sincere.

Without dwelling on it, I close the distance between us and catch her lips with my own.

Julia instantly melts into my embrace. I'm drunk off the taste of her, and I want more. I nip at her bottom lip, begging her silently for permission. Her mouth parts for me, and I swallow up her moans as my tongue dances with hers.

But even as we kiss, I can feel her body sinking more deeply into me, *through* me.

Reluctantly, I pull away. Her heated gaze catches mine as I take a step back. I know she can see that my form is no longer entirely solid, but it doesn't seem to scare her.

"I'm sorry," I breathe, inexplicably ashamed.

"This is why you said you wouldn't come with me, isn't it?" she asks. Her tone is gentler now and tinged with sadness.

I nod. "I only have power here in the swamp, and even that's limited," I say. "My spirit is tied to this place. If I leave, I'll fade away to nothing." It's a bleak reality, but it's the truth.

"But what about your grave? Can't you go to wherever the workmen reinter you?"

"It doesn't work that way," I sigh. "Those are just my bones, but this is where I died. Without a living body, my spirit can't leave. But you can, and you should." It breaks my heart to suggest it, but I won't be able to bear watching Amos tear her apart.

Julia sags down onto the couch. "I don't know what's right anymore, Zeke," she confesses. I sit down next to her, wishing I could do more to comfort her as she wrings her hands in her lap. "If I leave, I'm admitting that I made a terrible mistake in marrying Jake. But if I stay..."

"Didn't Helen's friend help you?" I'm genuinely curious. If there's a way to get rid of Amos for good, I want to know about it.

She tugs her purse off her shoulder and pulls something out of it. The object is a small, misshapen bottle filled with a dark liquid. It's sealed with a glob of red wax that's dripped and hardened down the sides of the glass vessel.

Intrigued, I ask, "What is it?"

"I'm not entirely sure," Julia murmurs. "Helen took me to see a Voodoo priestess. She gave me this potion. Apparently, it's supposed to bind Amos to whoever drinks it, and then that person's sacrifice will banish the demon."

A sour pit of dread pools in my gut. "Sacrifice? As in, somebody has to die?"

Julia buries her face in her hands and shakes her head. Through the gaps in her fingers, she mutters, "It's horrible, I know."

"Don't do it," I plead. Julia is so sweet and innocent. I don't think she'd ever be able to hurt anybody. If she's forced to choose somebody to die, even if it means getting rid of Amos, I think that would break her. The demon, and any sacrifice necessary to fight it, shouldn't be hers to shoulder.

"I don't think I can. Who would I even give this to? It's monstrous.

Besides, I don't even know if it'll work. Imagine poisoning somebody for some dumb Voodoo spell, all for nothing. I don't think I could live with myself," she rambles.

Her words offer me a good bit of relief. At least she's not seriously considering using the potion. I'd shudder to think what might happen if she did.

"Somebody else can deal with Amos," I tell her. "You've been through enough, and you owe it to yourself to get the hell out of here. Go back to New York or somewhere nice like Florida. Divorce Jake, and forget about me. Be happy."

"Zeke…"

"Just promise me you'll think about it," I insist.

She only pauses for a moment before offering a small, "Okay."

We sit in contemplative silence for a few minutes. After a while, Julia shifts on the couch so that she's lying down with her head in my lap. I have just enough strength left in me to comb my hand through her auburn hair, watching as the light plays of the coppery strands.

"How did you die?" Julia asks out of the blue.

I blink. It takes a moment to recall that day. The memory is fuzzy around the edges, yellowed like an old photograph.

"I was electrocuted," I reminisce finally. "A lot of houses in these parts didn't have power like they do these days. In remote areas, you'd have to be pretty rich to get the wiring done. The Gregory family had gone for years without it but finally decided it was time. I'd been one of three men to lay the original copper wires down. Only two were left by the end of the day."

"That's terrible!" Julia gasps. After a moment of contemplation, she follows up with, "What did it feel like? Dying, I mean, if it's not too awful of me to ask."

"After I got over the whole electrocution thing, it wasn't that bad," I shrug. "It was kind of nice actually. No taxes, no bills. But it gets boring after a while–and lonely."

Julia frowns. "But aren't there other ghosts here too?"

"Absolutely. You've heard the children, I think. They're a mischievous bunch. And Miss Penny's always around, keeping us all in line.

There are a lot more out in the swamp, but they tend to stick to themselves. I think it bothers them that the house doesn't look the way it used to," I explain. "Think of it like being stuck in a home with the same dozen people for a hundred years. We're all pretty sick of each other."

That gets her to crack a small smile. "And what was your life like before you ended up here?"

A pang of nostalgia hits me as I struggle to remember. "It was okay," I answer after a moment of thoughtful silence. "Life was nothing special, but it was mine. I'd come down from New Orleans. I'd followed a girl here, actually."

"A girl?" Julia repeats. Her interest is tinged with the slightest edge of jealousy, and that only makes me want her more.

"Don't you worry; she's long gone," I chuckle. "But she was very pretty and had a quick sense of humor. You remind me of her, actually. She'd come to Hahnville to take care of an elderly family member. I'd been quite taken with her so I'd found myself some work in construction out here, hoping that maybe we'd bump into one another in town."

"Did you?" she prods.

"No," I sigh. "It was only my second day on the job when it happened. I never did see her again."

Julia stares up at me sadly. "That's so tragic."

"It is," I agree. "But think about it. If I hadn't died in 1931, then we'd never have met."

"Silver linings," Julia murmurs.

She doesn't ask any more questions. Instead, she closes her eyes, clearly relishing the feel of my fingers weaving through her hair. After a while, her breathing evens out, and I realize she's fallen asleep.

Using up the last of my strength, I slip out from under her, taking great care not to wake her. I pull a crocheted quilt off the arm of the couch and spread it over her prone form.

Before I fade, I lean down and kiss her gently on the lips.

Even though she can't see me, I'll still be here watching over her.

I'll protect her, no matter what the future holds.

20

ANOTHER ALLY

Julia

It's bright when I wake up, and for a moment, I'm completely disoriented.

It takes a few seconds for me to realize that I'm lying on the couch in the living room. A throw blanket covers my legs, but there's no other sign of Zeke. Wasn't he just here?

I sit up and shake the sleep from my body. Even though the living room lights are on, I can tell that it's dark out. What time is it?

My purse sits on the coffee table in front of me alongside the vial of Mama Janvier's potion. Sickened by the mere sight of it, I slide the bottle back into my bag before fishing my cell phone out instead.

The clock on the lock screen tells me it's almost four in the morning. How had I slept so long?

Still groggy, I stand and pick my way into the hallway. The house is cool and dark. It strikes me that Jake should've been home by now, but there's no sign of him. Surely, he would have woken me if he'd come in late.

Maybe he's upstairs, already asleep in our bedroom.

I stop at the base of the steps, perching on the bottom one so that I can pull off my heels. I'm far too tired to go wobbling around on them in the dark. I leave them by the front door and pad up the stairs in my bare feet.

The second floor feels as vacant as the first. There isn't even the telltale sound of Jake's snoring to indicate that he's here.

Uneasy, I creep over to our bedroom. The door stands open, exactly as I'd left it earlier when I'd first gone down to greet Helen. When I peer inside, I know immediately that the room is empty.

"Where the hell is he?" I mutter as I step fully over the threshold. My hand gropes along the wall for the light switch. I find it and flick it on, illuminating the space with a warm glow.

I don't know whether I should be angry or worried. He'd assured me he'd be back later. Hell, he'd even turned on his location settings on his phone so I wouldn't have to wonder where he went.

The location settings! I'd forgotten about that entirely in the swirl of ghosts and Voodoo. I pull out my phone and open the tracking app.

My heart immediately sinks.

"A hotel?" I screech into the empty air. "That fucker's in a *hotel?*"

There's no disputing it, and there's no excuse for it either. In fact, it's like Jake *wants* me to know. Has he done this on purpose just to toy with me? Had he seduced me last night knowing that he was going to fuck some other girl tonight?

Cold rage wells inside of me as I spike my phone onto the bed. I want to scream, but I can't even bring myself to open my mouth. Instead, I'm simply frozen in the center of the room, seething.

I think back to how sweet Jake had been in the early morning hours of the previous day. He'd touched me so tenderly, so lovingly, that it almost physically hurt to think about. But then another image flashes through my mind, one of Zeke kneeling beside the bed, and realization strikes me like a bolt of lightning.

That hadn't been Jake, had it?

Somehow, it had been Zeke who had made such gentle love to me.

Hadn't he told me, speaking through Jake's lips, that it had just been a dream?

But that's what I want. Not somebody like Jake who uses me like a toy for his own whims and pleasure.

Zeke is my dream.

Longing surges through me as I think about the way he had worshipped my body so thoroughly. I want that again—more than anything.

But how can we ever have that? I'm alive and he's... not.

Even if I do somehow manage to banish Amos and divorce Jake, what then?

Zeke can't leave this place, which means I'd be stuck here too. It wouldn't be so bad, though, not with the demon gone and the man of my dreams by my side.

I allow myself a few moments to ponder that option, however improbable it may be. We could be happy, I think. Of course, it would be very different. For one, I'd grow old while Zeke would stay young as the years pass. But if we made sure I died on the property, wouldn't we be able to be together forever after that? I could handle that, as long as the hope of eternity glimmered like a promise at the end.

The fantasy cheers me up enough that I'm able to retrieve my phone from the bed. I type off one final message to Jake, and then block his number.

Don't bother coming home, asshole.

It's now almost five o'clock. I don't see any point in trying to get back to sleep. There are too many thoughts swimming through my head even after making the choice to cut Jake loose.

Instead, I decide to take a shower. I stand under the hot water and imagine what it would feel like for Zeke to be in here with me. How would he touch me? I allow one hand to wander south toward the apex of my thighs.

Zeke, using Jake's mouth, had brought me an explosion of incomparable pleasure. What would his fingers feel like, I wonder? My thumb brushes over my clit, and I sigh at the sensation.

As I trace my own slick heat with my fingertips, I can almost feel Zeke's ghostly hand guiding me. Is it actually him? Is he watching me right now as I finger myself under the steaming waterfall of the shower, moaning into the darkness?

I come hard on my own digits with his name on my lips.

He's the only one I want, and I need him to know it.

I clean up the evidence of my arousal quickly and then move on to lather my hair. Once I'm clean, I turn the shower off and grab a towel, wrapping it around me before I return to the bedroom.

As I pull on a yellow sundress, I hear several steps of small footsteps run past the bedroom door, followed quickly by a jovial giggle. This time, the sounds of the phantom children don't scare me. Instead, I can't help but muster up a thin smile. Maybe Zeke and I can adopt some ghost kids, I think sardonically.

I take my time drying and styling my hair before I carefully apply my makeup. I consider using concealer to cover the yellowing bruise that mars my delicate cheekbone but ultimately decide against it.

Why should I protect Jake by hiding the evidence of his actions? It should be his shame to bear, not mine.

By the time I'm ready, dawn has broken to reveal a tentative blue sky. I'm surprised to see movement in the swamp when I look out the window. For a moment, fear lodges in my throat as I assume it must be Amos, but further inspection reveals the familiar figures of the workmen milling about on the edge of the back yard.

The permits to drain the marsh must have finally gone through, I realize. I'll feel better once the muck recedes from the foundations of the house. Will the boundaries of the swamp impact Amos's power at all? It's a curious question, and I decide that I'll have to ask Zeke later on.

In the meantime, I think I'll go down and chat with the work crew. I've grown fond of the foreman. Maybe I'll even make a big pot of coffee for everybody. I'd rather the company than sitting inside mulling over Jake's betrayal.

I open the bedroom door and nearly have a heart attack.

"Oh, my God!" I yelp, jumping back from the threshold.

An old woman stands framed in the doorway. She's very small, and there's something overwhelmingly familiar about her. After a moment, I realize that she reminds me of the woman who sold us the house. Layla, wasn't it? And if this is a family resemblance, I have a pretty good idea who this is.

"Miss Penny?" I guess once I've gotten a hold of myself.

The elderly lady smiles and nods. "Pardon me for scaring you, honey. I just thought it might be time for us to meet."

"You're a ghost," I say flatly. Like Zeke, she appears to be solid, but I happen to know that Miss Penny passed several months ago. Plus, hadn't Zeke said she was still here?

"You're a very observant young lady," Miss Penny deadpans back, though I can sense the vein of humor running beneath her words.

I can't help the grin that spreads across my face at the departed woman's quick wit. "And you're very polite," I retort good-naturedly. "Have you come about Amos?"

"I have," she replies. "Zeke would have come himself, but I fear you've worn the poor boy out."

A blush rises to my cheeks as I think about exactly how I've depleted so much of Zeke's limited energy.

Miss Penny waves her hand dismissively. "Oh, modesty doesn't matter much to the dead," she scoffs. "Besides, we have more important things to discuss. Amos is growing stronger by the day. He'll come for you soon."

The warning sends a chill rolling through my limbs. "I don't know what to do," I confess. "I know I should go, but I want to stay. I want to fight, but there's a price."

"There always is," Miss Penny agrees. "Is it worth it?"

"I'm so torn. I want to be with Zeke more than anything, but I'm going to have to sacrifice somebody to do it," I admit softly. I'm ashamed to even say it out loud, and the worst part is that I don't know if Zeke would ever be able to forgive me if I went through with it.

"What do you have to do?" the ghost asks.

"A Voodoo priestess gave me an incantation," I tell her. When I recite it from memory, Miss Penny nods in recognition. Then I continue, "But it won't be enough. I have to use a potion to bind

Amos to somebody, and then banish both of them with the spell. I don't think the person who drinks the potion is meant to survive."

"What a terrible choice," Miss Penny sighs.

"Is there any other way to get rid of Amos?"

The spirit shakes her head. "Many have tried, and all have ultimately failed. Even I couldn't find a way, and you can believe me when I say that I had years to experiment."

"So this is it?" I ask her. "Leave–or lose myself?"

"This is it." It's not a comforting answer, but it rings true. "Whatever you choose, I'll do what I can to help. So will the others. We've endured Amos's chaos long enough. I'd like to see my home at peace."

Before I can ask her anything else, Miss Penny's form fades before my eyes until she disappears completely.

"I don't think I'll ever get used to that," I mutter as I step through the doorway where the old woman had just been standing. I half expect to experience a cold spot or eerie feeling where the ghost was, but the air feels normal and entirely undisturbed.

How many times have I walked directly through a ghost without knowing it? It's a rather unpleasant thought, and I push it away quickly.

My head is already spinning from the choice that looms over my head. It's all I can think about as I head downstairs and out the back door.

I stand on the porch and watch as the workmen mill around with strange pieces of equipment. It strikes me that I have no idea what draining the swamp actually entails or how long it's going to take.

Either way, I know now that there are some things down there that should stay buried.

Some things are better left alone.

21
GIVING IN TO SIN

Jake

How fucking dare she!

My car swerves dangerously on the rain-slicked drive, nearly spitting me off into the cypress trees that line the shoulder of the path. I consider that maybe I shouldn't have had that final shot at the hotel bar before getting behind the wheel, but the thought floats away as quickly as it comes.

None of this is my fault.

It's Julia's.

That bitch is the one who told me not to come home. You know, the home I fucking built for her.

I can't believe the level of disrespect she's shown me. I'll fucking show her what happens when she challenges me.

The path finally opens up into the wide, open expanse of the driveway. I can't seem to steer straight enough to confidently navigate into the garage, so instead, I haphazardly pull up at the front door. The pouring rain thunders on the roof of the car, drowning out the sound of the gravel beneath the tires.

I stumble out into the storm. Within seconds, I'm already drenched. Cursing loudly over a peal of thunder, I stagger through the darkness trying to find the front door.

Instead of the hard stone slab of the stoop, my shoes slide on slick grass underfoot. I'm confused for a moment, unsure of where I am. The backyard maybe? How'd I get all the way around the house?

I can barely see the building in the gloom. The alcohol I consumed earlier, along with the pills I'd popped in the bathroom of the hotel room when Ellie wasn't looking, pitch the world to spin around me. Even though my feet are moving, I have no idea where I'm going.

It's as if my body moves of its own accord. I'm powerless to resist the pull as my feet sink into increasingly soft ground. Mud sucks at the soles of my shoes. I feel like I'm slowly sinking in quicksand. Yet, I still move forward.

When I reach a patch of moss littered with a treacherous maze of long, narrow holes, I realize where I am.

Somehow, I've made it through the marsh to the clearing where the decayed cemetery once stood.

Amos is waiting for me there. Its form wavers in the rain, like a projection on a disrupted screen. It looks less human than I remember. The general form is there, but the angles and proportions are all wrong. For some reason, it makes me think of an anglerfish, drawing me in with the promise of a light in the dark.

"Rough night?" the demon asks in a voice that's merely an extension of the howling wind. It grins, revealing thin gleaming teeth that flash in the lightning like slivers of bone.

"That bitch didn't learn her lesson," I growl, struggling to be heard over the rushing rain.

"She didn't," Amos agrees. "In fact, she's forsaken you entirely."

"What?" My brain's too addled to make sense of the words.

Its smile grows impossibly wide. "She's been whoring around with another man. A ghost. Can you imagine a dead man fucking your wife while you're gone? I'd be furious."

A ghost? I don't stop to consider the logistics. As horrifying as

Amos is, the demon has never lied to me. If it says Julia's been running around on me, it's probably telling the truth.

"That fucking bitch!" I rage into the storm. My hands claw at the air in front of me, and I know that if she was standing before me right now, I'd squeeze the fucking life out of her.

"Now, now," the demon croons. "Let's have a little patience. If you confront her like that, the fun will be over far too soon. The ghost took you over before in order to fuck your wife. Did you even know that?"

"No," I grind out. If Amos is trying to sooth me, it's doing a terrible job. The thought of some asshole ghost possessing me and bending my wife over just adds fuel to the fire.

"Now, here's what you'll do," the demon instructs, ignoring my rage. "You go in and act sweet as molasses. Let her think you're her lover, Zeke. And when you've got her where we want her, you let me in."

"Let you in?" I slur.

Amos hisses in agreement. "Yes, yes, like before. Let me punish Julia for you, and, in return, I'll give you everything."

I narrow my eyes. The demon made good on its promise of securing me that last investor. Hell, I'd even gone out to celebrate that night, and for the next few days after. Everything is going smoothly now, but I could always use a boost in the industry. If Amos will give me that in exchange for my whore of a wife, who am I to argue?

"Deal," I say quickly.

"It's a deal!" Amos confirms gleefully. "Now go."

I'm barely aware of my surroundings as I wade across the sludgy ground and back toward the house. I hike up the lawn and across the porch to let myself in the back door.

Nothing moves inside the house. Rain blares against the windows as I creep through the first floor toward the darkened stairs. My muddy shoes leave a trail of murky footprints in my wake, marking my path as I journey upward.

Julia is asleep in bed, as I expected. Rage flares within me at the sight of her. How dare she look so peaceful, so content, when she's torn my life to shreds?

Patience.

Amos's voice slithers coolly across the contours of my mind, soothing my anger even as I think about Julia fucking somebody else.

The smallest worm of doubt wriggles in my gut. What if there is no ghost? What if Amos is lying? Is it possible that the demon could desire my wife so badly that it would do or say anything to get me to agree?

But that final tremble of uncertainty is snuffed out when her eyes flutter open to see me standing beside the bed.

"Zeke?" she murmurs.

Amos's grating laugh rips through the inside of my skull.

I told you. Now do as you promised.

I blink hard. What am I supposed to do? I can barely think with Julia staring at me like that with heat and questions brimming in her eyes.

Tell her you're him.

"It's me," I say dutifully. "Zeke."

The soft smile that spreads across Julia's face is pure torture. It takes every ounce of my self-control not to slap it off her.

"I thought you were out of energy," she muses as she sits up.

"I'll always have energy for you." I try not to look too pained as I say it.

Her eyes flicker down my body before she meets my gaze again. "Does Jake know? I mean, is he aware you're in there?"

I shrug. "Does it matter?"

Julia bites her lip as she ponders the question. Eventually, she responds, "Yes. He doesn't deserve to feel even a fraction of what we share between us."

My hands itch to strike her, but the cool fingers of Amos's presence hold me in check.

The pause is just long enough for Julia, unaware of my inner turmoil, to sit up on her knees. The fire in her eyes is unmatched, like nothing I've ever seen from her. It strikes me that she's never once looked at me like that in all the years we've been together.

"I'm glad you came back," Julia breathes as her hands move to gently brush the rain-slicked hair from my eyes. Confusion builds in her expression as she realizes that I've been outside. She opens her mouth to ask me a question that I won't be able to answer, so I do the only thing I can to shut her up.

I kiss her.

My lips are reluctant to meet hers, and I'm worried she'll realize that something is wrong, but she seems to interpret it as gentleness. I close my eyes, wanting this to be over.

Patience.

Amos's voice is a hiss in my mind, filled with promise. It urges me to kiss Julia back with as much passion as I can muster. The reward at the end will be worth it.

It has to be.

Julia's body is hot and slim against mine. As disgusted as I am right now, I'm still a man, and my body reacts accordingly, especially when one of her delicate hands skims over the front of my pants.

The sensation, even muted by layers of wet fabric, seems to breathe life into Amos. I can feel it seeping into my muscles and coursing through my veins. In a matter of seconds, I'm bursting at the seams with dark power.

Julia doesn't seem to notice the change in me. Her nimble hands make quick work of my fly, and she flashes me a sweet smile as she pulls my cock free from my slacks.

Her hot tongue presses against the blunt tip of my length, teasing me before her lips close over me as she draws me into her mouth.

Amos's presence surges through me. It's all consuming. My hands work of their own accord as they weave into Julia's hair and push her head roughly forward on my cock.

Realization blooms in her eyes as she stares up at me with wide eyes. She knows it's me now. She knows it's not Zeke.

"Is this what Zeke does to you?" It's Amos's voice that hisses out through my lips, its words that spark panic in Julia's face as the demon forces my cock deeper into her mouth. "Does he fuck your pretty face until you drown in his come?"

Julia's hands are on my hips. She pushes against me, struggling to get away, but my hold on her head keeps her locked in place. She can only endure as Amos's will guides me to pleasure myself in her mouth.

The more she squirms against my hold, the closer I get to release. I'm so lost in the pounding rhythm that I barely even notice as the phone in my pocket jolts to life to erupt a wavering, haunting melody. Julia's laptop, open but dark on the other side of the bed, blasts the same song, but the audio doesn't match up. The beats are uneven, the words crossing one another in a wretched dance.

...St. James Infirmary...

...Let her go, let her go, god bless her..."

The sound is maddening. I thrust faster, pumping my hips to the uneven gallop of the music.

And then finally, I tumble off the edge, emptying myself into Julia's mouth as Amos's unholy energy streams out of me in a shuddering release.

Julia finally pushes me off her and crawls back on the bed, gagging and coughing. Tears streak down her face. Her hair is a matted mess where I'd held her down on my cock.

It's only then that I realize what I've done.

Spears of guilt and shame pierce me, but I push them back. She deserved it, didn't she? After cheating? After what she's put me through?

I feel sick. The world spins as I try to focus on Julia, who's huddled pathetically on the other side of the bed.

When she speaks, her voice hits me like a punch to the gut.

"We're done," she whispers. "I want a divorce."

I blink heavily. For a moment, I think I'm going to vomit, but when I open my mouth to retch, a high-pitched laugh rings out instead.

Amos's laugh.

Julia's eyes widen in fear at the unhinged sound. She scuttles off the bed and launches herself into the ensuite bathroom. The door slams behind her, followed quickly by the lock clicking into place. But not even the cacophony that erupts from my throat is loud enough to drown out the sound of her tears.

I'm not sure how much time passes. At some point, I realize that I've simply stopped laughing. Disoriented, I use a discarded towel to haphazardly clean myself up before I tuck myself back into my pants.

My brain doesn't seem to be working properly. I can't seem to decide what to do next. But then I feel a tug behind my navel like there's a rope attached, and somebody's pulling, pulling, reeling me in.

I walk out of the room on numb, unsteady feet. I stagger down the stairs and out the front door, where the rain lashes against my skin in stinging curtains.

"Amos!" I howl into the night. "Amos!"

"No need to shout," a voice chides from just over my shoulder.

I whip around in surprise, expecting to see the horrendous form of the demon looming over me, but there's nothing there.

"Want do you want, Jake?" the disembodied voice queries expectantly. It seems to be coming from the very rain itself, from the stench of the swamp, from the muddy gravel under my feet.

I want to forget. I want to be anybody else. I want this nightmare to end.

"I want you to take her!" I scream into the storm. When Amos doesn't answer, I bellow, "You can have her! Do you hear me, you piece of shit? You can fucking *have her*!"

Two bony hands clamp down on each side of my face. Talon-like nails dig into my forehead as Amos's waxy face swims into view. It stops less than an inch from mine, so close that I can't possibly look away from the matte black pits of its eyes.

"Yes," Amos agrees, grinning. "I will have her. She will be mine."

I screw my eyes shut. I can't bear the sight of the demon in front of me any longer. "What do I have to do?" I ask weakly, all traces of my former bravado washed away with the rain.

"It's simple," Amos assures me. "All you have to do is let me take you over completely. And then you'll see. You'll see… everything."

I already know how I'll answer. My soul's already damned, anyway.

"Yes," I breathe. "Do it."

"She's mine," Amos croons as his fingers tighten over my skull.

The pain is blinding. I want to scream, but the air is stolen from my lungs. It's unbearable.

But over the agony, I can hear Amos's voice ringing through the night, repeating its promise over and over again.

"She's mine. She's mine. She's mine…"

And in my final moments of clarity, I think that maybe, just maybe, I've made a terrible mistake.

2 2

AN OPEN DOOR

Julia

It's over.

There's no room for doubt as I drive through the worst of the storm. I feel violated, all the way down to my soul. My face is red and streaked with tears, and my lungs constrict with every breath I take, as though my chest is trapped in an immovable vice.

Jake's actions are unforgivable.

And it had been Jake, not Zeke. I'm absolutely sure of that. Aside from the fact that Zeke would never treat me so horribly, we'd simply spent so much time together during Jake's absence that the ghost was all but drained of energy by the time my husband returned home.

But there was something else wriggling through the back of my mind, insidious and full of venom.

How had Jake even known about Zeke in the first place?

He didn't look at all surprised when I spoke the spirit's name aloud. In fact, he played along with it, lulling me into a false sense of security until the point of no return.

Only then did Jake reveal himself.

Somebody must have told him about Zeke. Somebody must have put him up to such a terrible charade.

"Amos." I gasp out loud as the pieces of the puzzle click into place.

My mind drifts back to that horrible moment when my husband's eyes flashed down at me with so much malice. His gaze was impossibly dark, almost black, in the moonlight, ripe with the demon's influence.

Horror blossoms in the pit of my stomach. How long has Jake been colluding with Amos? Does he even know that it's a demon?

"What have you done, Jake?" I choke out.

Part of me wants to turn back. Maybe I can help him. Even after everything he's done, he doesn't deserve to be left at Amos's machinations. Zeke had told me about some of the things the demon has done over the years. It shows no mercy and doesn't stop until its prey is dead. No matter how monstrous Jake has acted, it pains me to just leave him there.

But I can't go back.

I can't.

That certainty offers me little comfort as I navigate the rain-washed streets of Hahnville. Fat droplets splatter against the windshield, rendering visibility to nearly nothing. A quick glance at the illuminated clock on the dashboard shows that I've been driving in circles for over an hour. I don't even have a destination in mind.

After all, It's not like I have anywhere to go.

Fresh tears streak down my cheeks. I'll be out of gas soon, which means I'll have to stop eventually. There must be a motel or something where I can book a room. But then I realize that I fled the house without my purse, leaving me without a wallet, cards, or cash.

I want to scream. I want to pound my fists against the steering wheel, even though it will accomplish nothing.

I hate Jake. I hate Amos. Helen was right when she'd told me how terrible the demon was.

Helen.

Didn't my neighbor say that I could always ask her for help? As much as I hate to test her generosity, I don't really have much of a choice.

I turn the car around and head back toward the swamp.

A tentative wave of hope threads through my veins as I find the start of Helen's driveway about a mile down the road. A cheerful yellow mailbox with WILSON painted on the side in tall blocky letters marks the opening in the trees.

Panic sets in for a moment as the cypress branches close in over the car. It's so similar to our driveway that I can't help but feel that I've somehow taken a wrong turn, and that, at any second, I'll pull up into the open gravel expanse in front of the house.

But then the trees part, revealing Helen's home in all its comforting glory.

All the windows are dark, though the light on the porch is on. Helen's car is parked in the dirt space beside the house, alongside a well-loved red pickup truck.

I hesitate as I pull up behind the vehicles. It's so late, and the older couple is probably asleep. I don't want to bother them at this hour, but I have no resources and nowhere else to go.

Helen ends up making the choice for me. She must have heard my car because a light flashes on in one of the upstairs windows. By the time I'm out of the car and have sprinted through the rain to seek shelter beneath their covered porch, the door swings open.

"Julia?" the woman calls out. "Is that you?"

I nod as I step into the dim glow of the porch light. "I'm so sorry Helen, I just... I..." My voice trails off into a silent sob.

"Oh, honey, what's happened?" Helen gasps, wrapping her arm around me. She guides me toward the door and into the comforting safety of her home.

"Amos," I manage to choke out. "Jake..."

Even without much to go on, my neighbor seems to understand that something bad has happened. "You're soaked, sweetie. Let's get you into some dry clothes and have a nice warm drink, okay?"

It's all I can do to nod. Now that I'm somewhere safe, the reality of the situation comes crashing down on me all at once, bringing with it a wave of exhaustion so strong that I have to channel every ounce of my energy into following Julia upstairs.

She offers me a pair of her sweatpants and a T-shirt, which I accept gratefully, before leading me to the guest room.

"You take your time," she says kindly. "Just leave your wet clothes in the hamper in the bathroom. I'll take care of those for you. When you're ready, I'll have tea for us in the living room."

As promised, she ducks out to give me some privacy to change, and I'm once again left alone with my thoughts. Numbly, I strip off my soaked clothes, thankful for the small mercy that my panties are dry. I toss my gown into the hamper and then pull on the borrowed clothes.

Before I head downstairs, I do my best to freshen up in the bathroom. My hair is an absolute mess. I comb my hands fruitlessly through the tangled tresses before giving up entirely and use a hair tie I find on the sink to secure it into a loose ponytail. Once I've tamed my hair, I splash warm water on my face in hopes that it might take away from the puffy redness that rims my eyes.

It's as presentable as I'm going to get.

I pad out of the room in bare feet, trekking through the hallway and down the stairs toward the living room. Helen is already there, waiting for me on the couch. There are two steaming mugs on the coffee table, and she pushes one over to me as I sit down beside her.

"Thank you," I say as I gratefully accept the offered cup. The heat of the liquid seeps into my fingers and radiates through my palms as I clasp it in both hands.

"You're very welcome," Helen nods. "I put a dash of whiskey in yours. It looks like you could use it."

I offer her a watery smile. "I could use the whole bottle, honestly," I confess. "Helen, I'm so sorry to just show up like this. I know I must have woken you and…"

The older woman holds up a hand, cutting me off. "I told you that my door would always be open to you, and I meant it," she assures me. "I'm just glad you were able to get here instead of the alternative. Now tell me, what happened?"

I hesitate for a moment. Do I tell Helen that I've been growing more and more intimate with the ghost of one of Amos's victims? It's not that I'm worried she won't believe it. No, I'm more concerned that she'll judge me and think I'm terrible.

But I owe Helen, who's pulled herself out of bed to help me, the full and unadulterated truth.

"Jake is under Amos's influence," I finally reveal. "I'm not sure if Amos made him do it, or if Jake just did it on his own." My voice sounds so small in the room, so full of shame. "And I think, maybe… maybe I deserve what he did to me." I squeeze my eyes shut as tears track down my cheeks. I don't want to see Helen's reaction as I add, "Because I've been cheating on Jake with a ghost."

The following few seconds tick past in silence. I'm absolutely sure that Helen must think I'm a horrid person and is simply puzzling out some polite way to get me to leave.

I'm utterly shocked when I feel her arms wrap around me to pull me in for a warm, motherly hug.

"Oh, honey, you poor thing," she murmurs. "Whatever he did to you, you don't deserve it. I'm not sure what he expected you to do when he was off running around on you with half the women in New Orleans."

"So you don't think I'm terrible?"

"Of course not," she assures me. "I think you're a woman in a very tough situation, and you deserve to hold on to love when you can find it."

Her kind words usher in another bout of heavy sobs. It takes a while for me to calm down to the point where I can pull away and start to sip my tea. The smoky taste of the alcohol lingers in my mouth with each sip and spreads some much-needed warmth throughout my body.

"Do you truly believe that Amos has gotten to Jake?" Helen asks once she deems that I'm in a slightly better state of mind to answer questions.

"I'm sure of it," I tell her. "He was different, and he knew about Zeke. Only Amos could've told him."

Helen shakes her head. "This is bad. Very bad."

"What do I do?" My words drip with desperation.

"We perform the ritual," Helen replies firmly.

"No!" I blanche. "You heard what the Voodoo priestess said! Somebody is going to have to die, and I just… we can't do that. We *can't!*"

"If you won't use the potion, then we can at least weaken him with the incantation," Helen suggests. "We lure him into the swamp and do our best to end him."

"And if it doesn't work without the potion?" I counter.

Helen shrugs. "Then we'll probably die anyway."

It's not exactly comforting, but she's right. We have to try.

The older woman takes my hand and gives it a comforting squeeze. "We'll go tomorrow. I'll help in any way I can. I promise."

"Thank you, Helen." Although I don't want to put her in any danger, I'm glad that I won't have to do it alone. A thought occurs to me then, and I add, "What if I go back first? I can talk to Zeke and the other spirits. Maybe they'll help us too."

Helen offers me a thoughtful nod and agrees, "That might just be the edge we need."

Now that we've solidified our plans for tomorrow, Helen leads me back upstairs to the guest room. After exchanging good nights, my host retires back to her bedroom, leaving me alone with only my gnarled thoughts for company.

I crawl into the unfamiliar bed and wrap the covers tightly around myself. I'm so tired, but no matter how hard I try to fall asleep, my brain just won't let me. Instead, I find myself staring blankly up at the ceiling, thoughts racing through my mind before I can fully process them.

Are we really going to kill Amos tomorrow? And if we do, what then? I'll divorce Jake, that's for sure. Maybe then Zeke and I can have a life together.

But all of that hinges on destroying Amos.

And killing a demon won't be easy.

2 3

GANGING UP

Zeke

I'M GOING TO KILL JAKE.

It's all I can think about. I didn't have the energy to intervene as he hurt Julia and shattered their relationship beyond repair. I'd tried to manifest myself, to fight against Amos's hold on Jake, but it was no use.

I wasn't able to protect Julia.

I failed her.

A powerful surge of anger flows through me as I think about how distressed she was as she snuck outside, jumped into the driver's seat of Jake's car when he wasn't looking, and sped off into the rainy night. Even though I desperately wanted to go with her, I'm unable to cross the invisible line marking the boundary of the property. I can only hope that she's taken refuge somewhere safe, some place where Jake can't follow.

It's morning now, and there's no sign of Julia. Jake lays in the driveway amidst a mess of mud and gravel, unconscious. I'm itching to kick him, but I'm still too weak to summon my corporeal form.

Instead, I spare him a scathing glare as I bypass his prone form and head toward the swamp.

I feel Amos before I see him. Its gaze upon me is omnipresent, unwavering. I wade out through the receding mire and climb onto the mossy, pitted clearing where I'd once been entombed.

"Amos!" My challenge booms through the swamp. The underbrush rustles as small creatures startle at the sudden noise, and the trees whisper warnings amongst themselves. "Show yourself, you coward!"

For a moment, nothing happens.

But then the constant drone of insects ceases as though somebody simply hit pause on a recording. Nothing moves. Even the feathery leaves of the cypress trees freeze in a tense vigil; the very wind itself is holding its breath.

Amos appears in pieces, a patchwork of mottled shadows coalescing from the swamp. Its skin, paper-thin and the texture of tree bark, stretches taut over branching bones. The fine, dark hair reminds me of the soft ferns that grow in the shade of the cypress trees, feeding off the muddy decay of the marsh. It's an eldritch amalgamation of the land itself, drawn forth into the vaguest shape of a man.

I can't help but recoil in horror at the unnatural sight of it.

"Hezekiah," Amos murmurs in recognition. "How nice to see you again."

"You bastard," I growl.

The demon wags one long, thorn-tipped finger at me. "Is that any way to greet an old friend?"

Rage boils through me. Now that I'm standing in the swamp, I can feel the power coalescing inside me. It fans the dormant embers of my energy, recharging the spent wells that I've drawn so much from over the last few weeks. Slowly but steadily, my body manifests.

This new surge of strength gives me the bravado to warn him. "Stay away from Julia."

Amos's jagged mouth opens in a squealing laugh. I wince and slap my hands over my ears, but I can't block the sound out. It reminds me of twisting metal and the crash of an oncoming storm. When it ends, the whole swamp seems to shiver in relief.

"Julia is mine," the demon hisses.

"She's *mine*," I spit. "She'll never be yours."

"Oh, but it's already done." The words ooze from Amos's maw like mud. "Poor Jake, so full of sin. He was easy to convince. He didn't even struggle, not like the last stupid fool."

My eyes widen in terror. I knew that Jake was colluding with Amos by allowing the demon to ride around in his body and poison his mind. But after seeing the man sprawled out in the driveway just outside the front door of the house, I should have realized that a deal was already struck.

Thank God Julia made it out last night.

"You're too late," I goad him. Julia isn't stupid. There's no way she'll come back here after what Jake did, not even for me. And since I know she'll never be able to use that cursed potion on anybody, there's no reason for her to come back. A pang of sorrow strikes my heart as I realize that I might never see her again, but I push it away.

I'd rather love her for eternity from afar than to watch her meet her death at Amos's hand.

The demon laughs again, but I don't flinch this time. "She'll come back," it croons. There is no room for doubt in its tone, and I wonder if perhaps it knows something I don't. "She won't leave you, Hezekiah. She will come back for you, and her death will forever haunt your heart."

"Even if she does, I'll stop you!" I roar. My voice is confident and loud, but deep down, I'm not so sure. I couldn't even stand in Amos's way last night. Even with my power restored, can I really stop the demon from hurting the woman I've grown to love?

As though sensing my unease, Amos grins. "What do you think you can possibly do about it, dead man?"

I'll show it what I can do.

I swing my corporeal fist, aiming to shatter the demon's brittle bones and tear through that tree bark skin, but my knuckles sing only through air, hitting nothing.

Amos swirls together a few feet away, utterly unruffled.

A war cry tears from my mouth as I barrel toward it. What feels like adrenaline flies through my veins as I advance, ready to end Amos here and now.

My body tumbles forward into the muddy ground.

"You think you can strike me?" Amos taunts, its grotesque form appearing over me. I try to scramble to my feet, but the ground is slick and I can't get my feet beneath me. "You're a fool, Hezekiah! My physical form is this very swamp. Nothing can hurt me here."

An idea flickers to life at the demon's words. Maybe like this, Amos can't be touched. But what about when it's possessing Jake? Does harm to the host deal damage to the parasite? It's an interesting theory, but there's no way to test it right now.

"I will find a way," I grind out as I finally find my feet. "Whatever it takes, I'll put you down."

"You? You're nothing. Insignificant. A mere shade will never harm me."

A shimmer of movement behind Amos captures my attention. The spectral form of Miss Penny is just barely visible, and she's not alone. Small, blurry shapes the size of children cluster around her, along with a myriad of other shimmering ghosts. None of them are quite as strong as I am, but there's power in numbers.

"Maybe not just me," I agree, pointing to the assembled spirits. "But are you willing to take the chance on all of us?"

Amos pauses for a moment. I'm confident that it never thought that we would gang up on it like this. But the sad reality is that most of us have died because of it. Accidents, murder, suicide – Amos pulled the strings on all of them. As it's added to his collection of damned souls over the years, it's inadvertently created its own opposition.

We won't stand for Amos's corruption any longer.

A simple nod from me is all it takes for us to rush the demon. The shimmering mass of spirits surrounds it in an instant, tearing and rending at its pulpy skin until it lies in shreds before us. Amos shrieks once, then twice, and then falls completely silent.

Is it over?

I hardly want to believe it. A ragged pile of debris litters the moss where Amos stood only moments before. The other spirits, their energy completely spent, flicker out of view one by one until I'm the last one left. The whole time, the swamp holds its breath.

Is this it? Is Amos truly gone for good?

But part of me knows it's too good to be true.

Just as I'm about to turn and leave the demon's remains to rot in the mud, the pile begins to stir. At first, it seems like the gentle rustle could just be the result of a breeze, even though the air is as still and stagnant as a grave. And then, little by little, the movement intensifies until the debris is whirling in its own miniature tornado, swirling around with such intensity that I have to brace myself against the gusting force of it.

"No!" I cry. The wind swallows up my voice as it reaches a fever pitch, drowning out the rest of the swamp. I throw my arms over my eyes in an attempt to ward off the flying debris caught in the maelstrom.

And then, as quick as it came, it's over.

Panic and fear rush through me as I peer out over my shaking arms. I know what I'll find before I see it.

Amos stands before me, whole once again.

My heart plummets. I hoped that we had more power in numbers. I wanted it to work. I *needed* it to, if only so that Julia wouldn't have to face this thing alone.

I was wrong.

The demon is on me in a flash. Before I can even react, its spindly hand closes around my neck and thrusts me into the air, holding me there as if I weigh nothing. Its thorny claws dig into my throat, draining the little energy I have left. Its matte black eyes flash in the morning light as the thing regards me carefully.

"Did you really think you could stop me?" it snarls, squeezing my neck for emphasis.

Unable to speak, I simply glare in response.

"You're pathetic," Amos hisses. "You'll never win against me. Julia will be mine."

"Never," I choke out defiantly.

The demon barks out a horrid laugh. "Let me tell you what will happen, Hezekiah. I'll lure little Julia home with the promise of finding you. And once I have her in my grasp, I'll drag her out here to the clearing and fuck her to death in the swamp."

I thrash wildly against the demon's hold, but it's too strong. My power is waning after the earlier attack. The only thing allowing me to hold my form is the sheer rage that courses through my body at Amos's words.

"How does that sound?" it taunts. "And if you're lucky, maybe I'll let you watch."

"Fuck you!" I manage to roar.

The words sap the last of my strength. My corporeal body disintegrates in Amos's touch, and I am free once again.

I linger for a moment, seething with anger as I watch Amos stare at its empty palm.

"You'll never win," the demon repeats, its eyes finding me in spite of me lacking a body. "She's mine."

"Never," I vow.

But can I keep that promise?

The odds are not in my favor, but I have to try.

24

BACK TO THE SWAMP

JULIA

THIS IS A TERRIBLE IDEA.

Every nerve ending in my body screams for me to turn around, but it's way too late for that.

I'm already here.

The house on the edge of the swamp rises up before me, blotting out the overcast sky. Clouds the color of fresh bruises creep overhead, threatening rain. It's barely evening, yet the darkness is already encroaching.

There's no sign of Jake. I'd half expected him to be waiting for me in the driveway, but the whole place seems deserted. I can only hope that Amos is lurking out in the swamp and is unaware of my arrival.

I survey the building in front of me. It looks like years have passed since I was last here, though it's only been a few hours. It looks like it could crumble into the swamp at any moment.

The front door hangs open, as though it's been waiting for me this whole time. I approach it cautiously, scanning for movement within, but everything is still.

Waiting.

"It's just a house," I whisper to myself, though I know now that it's much more than that. Even so, the words give me the courage to slip inside.

Something must be wrong with the air conditioning because it's absolutely stifling. Sweat prickles at the nape of my neck and courses down the fine curve of my spine to dampen the back of my borrowed T-shirt. I'm still wearing Helen's clothes, and I've never felt so out of my element as I do now, creeping around my own house like the protagonist in some shitty horror movie.

Once it's clear that nothing is going to jump out at me, I walk over to the staircase and listen. There are no footsteps upstairs, nothing to indicate that anybody is here. Maybe Jake left and ran off back to Ellie.

I try to hold onto that idea, but I still find myself reaching into the pocket of my sweatpants to clutch at the small potion bottle resting within.

"Zeke?" I whisper up the stairs. My voice seems impossibly loud in the silence. For the first time, I realize that the white noise hum of the air conditioner is gone, making everything echo in the strangest way.

I feel a little bolder when nothing happens. I wander into the living room first and then the kitchen, calling quietly for Zeke as I go. But the spirit doesn't appear.

"Where is he?" I mutter as I return to the hallway.

This isn't part of the plan. I hoped to find Zeke and ask him for his help in defeating Amos. I never thought he wouldn't come when I called.

A peal of thunder rips through the silence, causing me to jump. It's a stark reminder that we're running out of time. Amos's powers have been growing steadily, and I can only imagine that he's even stronger now. And I have no way of knowing when Jake will be back. He's more likely to aid Amos than to help me. After all, he's made it abundantly clear that he doesn't love me enough to fight against the demon.

Uneasy, I find my phone in the bedroom and dial Helen's number.

"I can't find Zeke," I explain quickly in a hushed tone. "I think we have to do this without him."

"I'll be right there," Helen assures me. She wastes no time on pleasantries and instead hangs up immediately.

I decide to wait outside until she gets here. The house feels like a mausoleum, airless, claustrophobic, and reeking of the swamp. I turn around to head back outside and freeze.

Jake looms in the doorway, blocking my path.

Only, is it really Jake? Or is it Amos? He's swaying slightly. The undulation is almost hypnotic, but otherwise, he doesn't move.

"Jake?" I ask. My tentative voice echoes in the silence.

He cocks his head as his body stills. His eyes look so strange. His pupils are blown, giving the illusion that his irises have overtaken the whites entirely.

"Jake, is that you?" I repeat.

"I knew you'd come," he answers in a slow, slurred voice. His mouth moves oddly, as though he's not fully in control.

"Are you on something?" I gasp. I want it to be true, but deep down I know there's something far worse than coke in his system.

Ignoring my question, Jake says, "I've been waiting for you, Julia." He takes a step forward, and I find myself backing away from him down the hallway.

"Leave me alone," I warn as I try to maintain my distance from him. Something in me whispers that if I try to run, it's over. But I get the sense he wants me to bolt, that he's craving the chase.

I won't give him that satisfaction.

"Alone?" Jake parrots. "You'll never be alone again. You're mine, Julia. *Mine.*"

"I'm not yours," I spit. I know it's not a good idea to provoke him, but I can't help the visceral reaction that bubbles up inside me. "Why don't you go claim Ellie instead? Or one of your other girlfriends?"

Jake darts forward before I can even process the fact that he's moving. His open palm connects with my bruised cheek with a resounding crack. Pain slams through my face, momentarily blinding me. In that split second, Jake grabs me roughly by my wrists and pulls me to him.

"You're mine," he hisses.

I thrash against him, but his grip is like a pair of iron vices around the delicate bones of my wrists.

"Let me go!" I howl. "Jake, please, you're hurting me!"

My husband's face looms over me, and from this close proximity, I realize that his pupils aren't dilated. His eyes are completely black. It's like staring into the heart of a hungry, lightless void.

A sick grin spreads over his face. "Sorry, sweetheart. Jake no longer lives here."

It's my husband's voice, but the words belong to Amos.

"No!" I gasp.

"Jake's already given himself to me," Amos croons. "And you're the price he agreed to pay."

"Zeke!" I scream. My voice ricochets off the shadowy walls. Where is he? He's the only one who can help me now.

Amos lets out a horrible, grating laugh. "Hezekiah can't save you," it taunts. "I'm going to have you, Julia. I'm going to fuck you until you beg me to kill you."

A bubble of fear bursts inside me, lending me strength. I shove Amos with everything I can muster. It stumbles back half a step, and its grip loosens just the tiniest amount, but it's enough. I jerk my arms away, breaking free from the demon's hold.

With nowhere else to go, I turn and run toward the back door.

I'm almost there, free and clear. But then a snarled hand tangles in my hair and yanks me back. I yowl in pain at the sudden harsh tug on my scalp. Amos, not wanting me to get away, wraps an arm around my waste, pinning me to Jake's body.

Amos opens its mouth to say something, but then it freezes. The eyes clear for a moment, and I'd recognize that honeyed shade anywhere.

"Zeke?" I breathe, hardly daring to believe it.

"Run!" Zeke yells through Jake's mouth.

I have a split second to dart away before the eyes cloud over once more, and Amos is back. At the same time, some unseen force crashes into the wall of the hallway beside me. The drywall caves, sending up a plume of dust that momentarily outlines the familiar shape of Zeke.

He staggers out of the hole and plants himself between Amos and me. Even though he can't speak, his message is clear. He'll hold Amos off. I just have to get to the swamp.

I have to do the ritual.

It's the only option.

Ignoring the throbbing pain in my wrists and cheek, I scramble through the hallway and burst out onto the back porch.

It's raining now. Droplets sting the tender flesh of my face as I try to keep my footing on the slick grass of the backyard. A ribbon of lightning curls across the sky, momentarily throwing the outstretched branches of the cypress trees into stark relief against the roiling clouds. A second later, a deep roar of thunder erupts overhead.

I instinctively know where I need to go to perform the ritual.

A good portion of the swamp has already been drained, leaving behind a vast field of bare land. The storm has churned the ground into thick mud that threatens to suck me under with every step. I lose one of Helen's borrowed flip flops to the primordial ooze, and then the other, but I continue forward. The whole time, I keep my fingers wrapped securely over the potion bottle in my pocket.

I hope to God the incantation works, but now, after feeling Amos's power first hand, I fear that it won't be enough. If I want to stop the demon for good, I'll have to use the potion.

But still, I wouldn't be able to live with myself if I made somebody else drink it. That leaves only one option.

I'll have to be the sacrifice.

It's the only way.

Tears brim in my swollen eyes. The rain snatches them mercilessly away before they can fall. I'm knee deep in mud, wading against a veritable tide of sludge. My hair clings to my skull and soaks my clothes, but I don't stop.

I can't stop.

I can see the clearing in the center of the swamp where the tomb-stones had once stood. It's strange to think that Zeke's bones had lain there, undisturbed, for almost a hundred years. But now his grave is a distant, vacant pit, unmarked and forgotten as its occupant once again wanders this property.

The old cemetery is so close. It's only about twenty feet away. I can make it. I *have* to.

Just as hope starts to well in my chest, a strong arm circles my waste, dragging me backward. I stumble clumsily in the mud as a second hand grasps my neck, forcing my head back.

"Did you really think you could get away from me so easily, Julia?" Amos grins.

My eyes search wildly for Zeke, but there's no sign of him. There's only Jake's body at my back, though I know that the demon is the one pulling the strings.

"Nothing to say?" it smirks. "No last words?"

I squirm in its hold, trying desperately to break free of its cruel arms. It's flush against my body, holding me so tightly I can barely breathe.

"I like it when you struggle," Amos hisses. Its tongue courses down my neck, and I have to suppress the urge to gag at the sensation. A roll of its hips shows me just how much it's enjoying the fight.

No.

It can't end like this.

I squeeze my eyes shut as Amos's hands start to wander over my body. With every rough touch, he utters the strangest words, releasing a haunting melody into the wind.

Folks, I'm goin' down to St. James Infirmary,

See my baby there,

She's stretched out on a long, white table…

Amos leans its head down until its lips are level to my ear. When it sings the next line, my legs fold beneath me in fear.

So sweet, so cold, so fair.

25

FIGHT FOR DOMINATION

Zeke

I'M NOT STRONG ENOUGH.

After Amos tossed me like a rag doll from Jake's body, I barely have any energy left. Still, I won't stop until there's nothing left of me. I have to fight for Julia. I can't let Amos take her.

As Julia runs outside into the storm, I square up to the demon. It's wearing Jake's body like an ill-fitting suit. While it's clumsy and unco-ordinated, its movements are still powerful.

"I told you not to get in my way, Hezekiah," Amos growls. It doesn't seem in any rush to chase after Julia. What game is it playing? Whatever it is, I don't want to find out.

"I won't let you hurt her." I stand firm, unwavering beneath its midnight stare.

"I will destroy you," the demon threatens as it stalks forward. "I will devour your very soul."

I parry to the side as it attempts to dart around me, blocking it from pursuing Julia's retreating form. "You can't kill somebody who's already dead," I snarl.

Amos laughs. The sound is something that a human throat shouldn't even be able to produce, and yet it rolls like a tsunami from Jake's slack mouth. That horrible noise drowns out my thoughts as Amos rushes forward and barrels into me.

The impact sends me sprawling to the floor. The demon steps over me, sparing me one contemptuous glance as it spits, "There are some things worse than death. Once I'm done with Julia, maybe I'll show you."

And then Jake's body slouches out the door, toward Julia.

I lay paralyzed for a long, terrible moment. I barely have any energy left. The sounds of Amos pursuing Julia are blotted out by the storm, but I have no doubt that he's after her.

And there's nothing I can do.

"Zeke!" A familiar voice draws my attention away from the back door and into the shadowy depths of the hallway.

Miss Penny manifests a few feet away. Fear creases her features as she comes to kneel beside me.

"Zeke, you have to get up," she insists, tugging at my arm. But her hands slide right through me. I'm barely visible, let alone solid.

"I can't," I pant, shame welling inside of me. "I've got nothing left."

The elderly shade's eyes grow hard. "You're the strongest out of any of us. You have to go after her. You have to stop Amos."

I squeeze my eyes shut and shake my head. I can't face Miss Penny, not when I'm so pathetic and useless. All I want to do is go after Julia and tear Amos limb from limb, but I can't.

Once again, I've failed.

"Look at me, Zeke," Miss Penny says sternly.

Reluctantly, I do as she asks.

Her face is alight with determination. "If energy is what you need, I'll give you mine," she says. "In fact, we'll all help."

Even though I can't see them clearly, I can feel the thrum of power as the ghosts of the old Gregory place gather behind her. The faces of Amos's many victims swim out of the darkness. I know what it will mean if they do this.

They'll no longer walk the halls of the house on the edge of the swamp.

"Miss Penny, I can't ask that of you," I breathe.

"There's no other option," she insists. "Amos bound the others here, and they're all about ready to move on. Use our energy to kill the demon, and set us free."

She gives me no time to argue. Instead, her hands plunge into the front of my incorporeal chest, finding my heart. Electricity zaps between us, burning through my veins with the force of the storm that rages outside. One by one, the spirits behind Miss Penny also reach out, offering me their power.

One by one, I drain them completely.

Finally, only Miss Penny is left. I'm bristling with power, but still she pushes the force of her own being into me. Her form fades before my eyes as I grow stronger, more solid.

"Thank you," I whisper as the last vestiges of energy trickle into me.

Miss Penny offers me one final smile. "It's time somebody around here rests in peace."

And then she's gone.

I'm alone.

There's no time to grieve the loss of the spirits who have walked with me for the last century. Pushing back the pall of sadness, I jump up and tear off into the night, following in the wake of Julia and Amos. I can only hope I'm not too late.

I can't find them at first. Sheets of rain cascade from the heavens, warping my surroundings. But then I hear the faint words of a song floating eerily on the wind.

I'm goin' down to St. James Infirmary...

The voice is coming from the swamp, from Amos.

"Please," I beg into the night as I slide across the backyard and launch myself into the mess of the partially drained marsh. "Please. Please, don't let me be too late to save her."

My feet, more solid than they've ever been since I'd resided in my living body, sink deeper into the mud with every treacherous step. I've only gone a short distance when I finally catch sight of Amos and Julia grappling out near the clearing.

"Julia!" I bellow, but she doesn't seem to hear me. Instead, the wind whips my voice away until the words are lost in the storm.

I lunge forward, tackling Amos down into the mud. Julia slips free of its grasp and struggles forward even as the demon regains its footing.

"Go!" I cry. I claw at Amos's legs, trying desperately to hold it back. But it dances easily out of rage, stopping only to grab a thick tree branch that has come down in the storm.

It advances steadily on Julia, who's solely focused on wading through the mire in a final effort to reach the clearing.

Mustering my newfound strength, I fly forward to intercept Amos before it can strike.

But the demon is too quick.

It lifts the cypress branch high in the air and then cleaves it downward in one swift motion. The wood cracks against the back of Julia's skull with an audible thud, and she crumples forward into the mud.

When the demon raises its arm to bring down another decisive blow, I realize that I only have one option left.

I've got to jump Jake's body.

The process is like forcing myself through a keyhole. Jake is there, but his mind is passive and yielding. I'm not sure if he's even aware of what Amos is doing. The demon must be placating him somehow, showing him a pleasant vision in stark contrast to the hellish events that are unfolding around him in reality.

And then there's Amos, lashing against me in a dark tidal wave, forcing me backward. The pain is intense, but when I scream, the sound erupts from Jake's mouth.

I've done it.

I'm in control.

Time is of the essence now. Even as I work the joints of Jake's body and push him forward, Amos is still struggling for dominance. Its efforts are draining my energy quickly.

Straining against the demon's influence, I go to Julia. Relief floods through me as I see that she's conscious, though only barely. Blood darkens her auburn hair, but the bump doesn't look too bad. I gather her from the mud and lift her gently in my arms.

At first, she thrashes, thinking I'm Amos.

"I've got you," I soothe as I stagger forward toward the clearing. "Just hang on."

"Zeke?" she mumbles skeptically. "Is that you?"

"For now. I'm not sure how much longer I can hold Amos off." Every step through the mud is agonizing, and the demon's voice rings through my head like a death knell.

Let me in.

LET ME IN!

"The cemetery," Julia murmurs. "The potion…"

The potion? Does she really intend to use it? The thought makes me shudder.

But if she doesn't, she will surely die.

I've got no choice but to continue toward the mossy clearing. Amos's power seems to grow as I gain ground, threatening my already tenuous hold on Jake. I try to focus on the weight of Julia in my arms, the feel of her skin against mine. It's the only thing that gives me the strength to continue.

I'll take her. She's mine. You can't fight me.

LET ME IN!

I shake my head against the demon's incessant thoughts. It's tearing at my mind with razor sharp talons, depleting my energy with each violent strike. But I don't give in. I have to keep going, just for a little bit longer.

"We'll make it," I whisper down to Julia. "I won't let Amos win this. We're almost there."

She peers up at me, squinting through the rain. Her eyes are bleary, but that can't disguise the steely conviction in her gaze. "Amos will never have me," she vows. "It might as well drown me in the swamp."

I open Jake's mouth to reply, but I never get the chance to speak. A surge of darkness overtakes me, ejecting me painfully from the man's body and back into my formless being.

Amos has wrestled back control.

"Fine," it sneers through its chosen vessel. Julia jolts at the word, recognizing that the demon has once again invaded Jake's mind. "I'll claim you here in this very swamp, the place you hate so much. And when your body finally breaks beneath me, I'll toss you into the water and watch you sink deep into the mud."

"No!" Julia howls. She twists in its grip to try and get away. With twisted hands, it clutches at her. But Julia is covered in the slick mud of the marsh, which proves to be surprisingly helpful as she slides heavily out of its grasp and onto the ground.

She tries to stand, but her movements are sluggish. Amos lets out a thunderous laugh that rings out through the rainy night like a peal of thunder.

"Do you really think you can run from me?" it taunts as it reaches for her.

Maybe Julia can't run, but I certainly can. I manifest my corporeal form as I throw myself between them, blocking Amos from hooking its fingers around its target.

"Enough!" Amos snarls. It twists its outstretched hand into my chest, firmly grasping the ghost of my heart.

"No!" I scream, but it's too late.

With one tug, Amos drains me almost completely.

My corporeal form blinks out of existence in an instant. I immediately throw myself at Amos in an attempt to regain control of Jake's body, but I'm no match for it anymore. I'm only in for a split second before it easily flicks me out again.

So I can only watch in helpless horror as the demon strides after Julia. It closes the distance between them quickly. Before she can react, it grabs her and slings her over its shoulder as though she weighs nothing at all.

"Zeke!" she shouts over the storm.

"Hezekiah can't help you now," Amos relishes. "Your lover will only be able to watch as I fuck you on what used to be his grave."

The worst part is, Amos is right.
There's nothing I can do.
Julia is already lost.

26

THE SACRIFICE

JULIA

THE WHOLE WORLD SPINS.

The driving rain is relentless, sloughing down my skin in cold rivulets. My hair hangs limply in a sodden curtain around my face, blocking my view of everything except the swirling muck below. There's a rank taste in the back of my mouth, and I understand dimly that I must have bitten my tongue when Amos hit me.

The place where the branch slammed into my skull throbs with every step the demon takes. Even though I can't see it, I'm pretty sure that I'm bleeding. My vision swims as I'm drawn deeper into the swamp.

"I'm going to break you on your husband's cock," Amos croons as it carries me over its shoulder like a sack of potatoes. "I'm going to fuck you until you plead with me to release you from your sorry life."

There's nothing I can do to block out the filthy, horrible things that spill from its twisted mouth. Instead, I fight against its hold, kicking my bare feet into the torso of Jake's body and pounding my fists against its back.

But my efforts don't seem to slow it down. To my horror, it seems to enjoy the way I struggle. Its fingers dig into the soft flesh of my thighs tight enough to bruise.

I know where the demon is taking me.

I recall how the foreman told me about the strange engraved rock the workmen dredged up from the swamp. They found it in the old cemetery as they'd been digging up the grave markers and the ancient bones that lay beneath. According to the Voodoo priestess, that rock might have been how the Gregory family summoned Amos–Asmodeus–in the first place.

Amos came from the clearing, and now it's taking me there, to the place where it has the most power. And there's nothing I can do to stop it from reaching its destination. The more I resist, the tighter its grip becomes.

In a last ditch effort, I claw at my pockets in an attempt to grab the potion. I can feel the small bottle against my hip, but I can't reach it.

Part of me is relieved. Even if I could get to it, would I really be able to drink the contents of the vial? If Amos does kill me as it intends, would my death trigger the spell? There are too many questions, too many unknown variables.

No, the potion isn't an option. I'm just going to have to fight the best I can and hope for a miracle.

It isn't until it climbs up onto the mossy clearing that it finally releases me. It throws me down on my back, knocking the wind out of me. I gasp and sputter desperately for air as it sinks down on top of me, straddling my hips. I can feel its hot excitement through the thin layers of fabric between us, and the sensation fills me with dread.

"You're mine, Julia," the thing hisses as it dips its face low over mine. A flash of lightning crackles overhead, reflecting hellfire in the matte black depths of its eyes.

"I'll never be yours," I snarl back. The weight of Jake's body pins me down. I can barely move. But I won't let Amos break me, not while I still have hope.

The demon grins. "You already are."

Disgust and terror bubble up in my very soul as it closes the distance between us and swoops in for a brutal kiss. My hands claw at its chest to push it away, but it's no use. Amos is too strong.

But I'm not powerless.

I find Jake's lip with my teeth and bite down–hard.

"You bitch!" the demon howls as it jerks back. Its hands fly to its mouth to cradle its wounded lip. Blood, glistening almost black in the darkness of the storm, dribbles down its chin and falls with the rain onto the front of my sodden, muddy shirt.

Amos's shock and pain seem to have given Zeke the opening he needs. The darkness clears from Jake's eyes, if only for a moment.

"Keep fighting!" Zeke instructs. "I need you to know how much I…"

Jake's head shakes violently, and when it stills again, the eyes are once again brimming with shadow.

"Your little boyfriend is quite troublesome," Amos growls down at me. "I'm going to make him watch as I tear your cunt apart, and then I'll crush him like the cockroach he is."

Its hands are on me again, tugging violently at my clothing. Just as the fabric of my shirt starts to rip, something swings out of the darkness and clocks Amos squarely on the back of its head.

Jake's body collapses down on mine. I cry out in pain at the sudden weight, but he's quickly rolled off of me.

My eyes search the darkness for my savior, but I don't have to look for long.

A harsh white light clicks on above me, revealing Helen.

The old woman's face is grim. She's holding a heavy flashlight, the kind somebody might keep in their car for emergencies. Dark blood and strands of hair stain the bottom portion of the lens, and I realize that Helen must have hit Amos with it, stunning him.

She reaches out a hand to help me up, and I take it gratefully. My head swims as she pulls me to my feet. Bile rises in my throat at the jerky movement, but I swallow it down.

"That was a close call," I pant as I struggle to catch my breath.

"It's not over yet," Helen warns as she shines the light down on Jake's twitching form. "We need to do the ritual. Now."

I nod. We're out of options.

Amos has to die.

I grope around in my pocket until my fingers close around the cool, textured glass of the bottle. Thank God it hadn't broken in the struggle. I extract it carefully and hold it up in the glare of the flashlight. The murky liquid sloshes within and I wrinkle my nose. It looks like it tastes terrible. I'm not looking forward to drinking it.

But I know what I have to do.

Using my nails, I scrape away the seal at the neck of the bottle and then work out of the stopper. The cork breaks free with a small pop.

"Bottoms up," I cringe, holding up the bottle in a mockery of a toast.

"Julia, no!" Helen catches my arm before I can drink. "What the hell do you think you're doing?"

"It has to be me," I insist. "There's no other way!"

She shakes her head. "I'll drink it. I've lived a good long life. If killing Amos is the last thing I do, then I'll die happy."

"Absolutely not," I argue.

Down in the mud at my feet, Jake groans. Both of us eye him warily. It isn't clear if Amos is still in control of his body, but I don't want to find out. And something tells me that's exactly what will happen if he wakes up.

"We don't have time for this, Helen," I sigh. Jake could regain consciousness at any moment, and then we'll be screwed.

A hard look passes over Helen's face. "You're right," she agrees. "I shouldn't drink it. But neither should you. Give it to Jake."

"What?" I gasp.

"Let Jake drink it. Hasn't he hurt you enough?" She scowls down at him, contempt plain on her features. "Is he really worth dying for?"

"I can't," I whisper in horror. "It would be wrong."

But that's not entirely true, is it?

Jake has hurt me. He's cheated on me, and he's struck me more than once. But the worst part is that he sold me out to Amos. Zeke told me that the demon could only possess a body for that long if the host agreed to a deal. And what had Jake promised it?

Me.

Cold rage writhes through me. Maybe Helen's right. Maybe he does deserve this.

Jake groans again, and my resolve waivers. How could I even consider sacrificing him?

His eyes flicker open, and in the washed out glow of the flashlight, I'm shocked to realize that his eyes are neither black nor amber. They're just normal.

"Jake?" I exclaim.

My husband blinks slowly, like a man waking from a dream. "Julia?" His voice is broken, almost inaudible above the roar of the rain.

I squat down beside him, the bottle in my hand momentarily forgotten. "I'm here," I reassure him. For all the hate that I hold for him, he's still my husband, and I can't bear to see him suffer.

"I'm... sorry," he murmurs.

A sob escapes my lips at his words. I know in my heart that he means them. He really means them.

He raises a shaky hand and points to the bottle clenched in my palm. "Let me," he urges.

It takes me a moment to realize what he's asking. I shake my head, causing pain to radiate from the spot where the branch had struck me. "No, Jake. I can't let you do that. You'll *die!*"

Jake grins. It's not the inhuman grimace of Amos, but the slick, confident smile that my husband dons when he's securing a business deal. "I'm already... dead," he forces out. It's clear that it's taking him great effort just to speak. "Let me... show you... how sorry I am."

Tears roll down my cheeks, mingling with the rain and the mud of the swamp. I don't want to do this. I really don't.

A cold, shaking hand closes over mine, working the bottle out of my grasp. Jake's movements are weak, and I could throw him off easily, but I don't. I simply let him take the vessel from me.

"I love you."

It's the last thing he says before he brings the neck of the bottle to his lips and drinks deeply.

I expect him to spasm or foam at the mouth as soon as he swallows, but he remains still in his crumpled position in the mossy clearing. I clasp my hands over my mouth, holding in my sobs.

I never wanted this.

I never wanted any of this.

"Julia?" Helen's alarmed tone jolts me from my stupor. "Julia!" She points down at Jake, who's still staring at me.

But now, his eyes are black.

"You fucking bitch!" Amos roars. It springs to its feet with surprising speed, causing Helen and I to flinch back. There's no time to dodge as its grasping hands reach out and grab me by one arm, pulling me toward it.

"Go back to hell!" I shriek as I push it away.

Amos stumbles, and as it does, something stirs deep inside of me. Unbidden, the incantation that Helen and the Voodoo priestess taught me rings through my mind.

Something ancient unfurls within me.

It's time.

I open my mouth and start to chant.

"From light to shadow, from stone to bone…"

A thread of lightning cracks open the sky overhead, and I feel the power of it radiating up from the mossy clearing and into my bones.

"I send you back to the void you've known!"

Amos yowls in pain. Its body jerks unnaturally like a marionette on tangled strings as it thrashes against some unseen attacker.

"By earth, by sky, by sea, I proclaim…"

The demon's eyes fix on me. The hatred in its gaze burns, but the power that swirls within me is too great.

"Be gone, demon, in darkness remain!"

At the final word, I rush forward and shove Amos as hard as I can.

For a split second, time seems to stand still. It teeters on the edge of the clearing, its arms reeling useless in the air.

And then Amos falls backward into the swamp.

As soon as it hits the mud, the brackish slime whirls up around it like the tentacles of some great beast. It pulls at Jake's limbs, dragging his body deeper and deeper into the mire. The demon's mouth opens in a soundless scream as the muck closes in over its lips, and then its nose, and then those horrible black eyes.

And then Amos is gone.

Amos is *gone.*

I know it in my soul.

As if a switch is flipped, the rain tapers off into nothing. For a moment, there's only silence. But then the crickets begin to whir deeper in the marsh, and the frogs start to bellow and peep in the underbrush. The whole place feels different.

Empty.

I step carefully to the edge of the clearing and peer down into the dark murk beyond. There are no bubbles in the mud, nothing that would indicate that Amos is still alive.

Or that Jake survived.

Helen comes up beside me and wraps a comforting arm around my shoulders.

"I think I just murdered my husband," I whisper to her. My voice seems too loud out here now, and I cringe at the sound of it.

The older woman shakes her head. "You're not responsible for this," she assures me. "This was his choice. Jake chose to save you in the end, even after everything he's done."

"He's dead," I say numbly. "Everybody will think I killed him."

"It'll be all right. And if anybody asks, I'll attest that it was self-defense."

I appreciate Helen's support, but it's not enough.

Like the stench of the swamp, Jake's death will haunt me forever.

Amos will torment me even from the depths of hell.

2 7

SO THIS IS DEATH

Jake

FOR ONCE IN MY LIFE, I'M ABSOLUTELY SURE I'VE DONE THE RIGHT thing.

I can't believe that I fell for Amos's empty promises. Even now, I wonder how much influence it exerted over my mind and actions.

Every shout, every slap, every nasty thought about Julia swims through my brain as my soul is torn to pieces. How much of that was Amos? I shudder to think about how much was me.

Because I do hold a hell of a lot of blame, don't I?

None of this would have happened if I'd been stronger.

But I was weak, and now, I have a terrible feeling that Amos knew that from the start.

As soon as I struck that deal in the driveway, Amos invaded my mind. The process itself was horrible. My brain and body was only big enough for one soul. The ordeal of adding another passenger was unbearably painful, and though my memories are hazy, I'm pretty sure that I passed out.

187

At first, it wasn't so bad, not after that first part. Amos promised me anything and everything, and I had stupidly believed it.

It wove me a nice, cushy dream. I was in that sky high office it showed me before. In my groggy, confused mind, I was utterly convinced by the illusion. I spent an indeterminable amount of time at the huge, glossy desk directing a staff of phantoms. I didn't suspect a thing.

Ellie had been there too. Amos pulled her form from my mind and made her my secretary. Her presence was distracting, to say the least.

But the more time I spent wrapped in the blissful arms of this vision, the more I realized that something wasn't right.

Strange aches and pains blossomed in my limbs, even though I wasn't doing anything more strenuous than lounging behind my desk. My voice grew more and more hoarse. And there was a headache that grew slowly but steadily over time until it reached a fever pitch that I could no longer ignore.

Yet, I didn't fight it. I wasn't strong enough.

The illusion only broke at the arrival of somebody new.

My head felt like it was splitting open. I slumped over the desk, moaning in pain as a strange presence forced its way into my mind.

The thoughts that come to me then were fractured snippets of what was happening outside.

My own body, but the eyes empty and black as pitch. Julia, wearing an unfamiliar pair of sweatpants and a ratty T-shirt, something she would never be seen dead in.

The feelings of love and concern for Julia came as the biggest surprise. They were overwhelming, moving me almost to tears.

All at once, I realized that this newcomer must be Zeke, the ghost Amos told me about, the one who stole my wife from me.

I expected myself to be overcome with anger, but the intensity of the dead man's love for Julia shocked me to my core. I felt something like that for her once, back when we were first dating. But as the years dragged on, that adoration shrunk to fondness, then to apathy before finally slipping into hatred under Amos's expert tutelage.

And in that moment, I realized that I no longer deserved Julia.

Maybe I never had.

Amos wrested control back from Zeke pretty quickly, but the damage was already done. The illusion was broken. And even though the demon fought hard to keep me totally in the dark, I was able to observe most of Zeke's view of the world unfiltered.

He forced me to watch Julia's fear and desperation. She said something about a potion, which was strange. What was she talking about?

Zeke's determined thoughts soon gifted me that insight. The potion had the potential to get rid of Amos for good, but that victory would come at a steep price. The ghost suspected that, with no other option in the face of certain death, Julia would use it on herself.

Amos would perish, but so would Julia.

I began to fight then. I was weak, far less powerful than Zeke had been against Amos's iron grasp on my body, but I tried. It wasn't much use, not until pain flared at the base of my skull and drove the demon out.

Momentarily freed, my path became clear. My body was largely intact, but Amos's and Zeke's grapple for control ripped my mind apart. And the damage to my soul? Well, I did that to myself.

I drank the potion.

I saved Julia.

Even if there's no absolution for me at the end, at least I was able to do that one thing, right that one last wrong.

And now, I sink down into the unrelenting darkness and await judgment.

Putrid mud closes in around me. Even with my eyes squeezed shut, I can feel the grit trying to claw its way between my lids. I try to keep my mouth closed, but I can't escape the fetid taste of it as it invades my nostrils. My lungs burn. I'm trying to hold my breath, delaying the inevitable.

There's a tearing sensation in some deep part of me, somewhere that transcends my body and dives into my very being.

It's Amos, I realize. The demon is ejected, shrieking, into the muddy void.

At last, I'm free.

As I, too, separate from my body and begin to descend, something shifts in the murk below us.

An eerie red glow filters through my field of vision, bringing with it a searing heat.

Hell, I realize dejectedly.

But is that really any surprise?

All of the terrible things I've done flash through my mind. Using women like objects to cheat on Julia, whose only sin was to love me in the first place. Building a business on a foundation of exploitation and greed. Slapping my wife.

Selling Julia out to Amos.

The portal below sucks me down, and I don't try to fight it.

Amos, too, is pulled deeper, but it doesn't go quietly.

Bursts of strange memories pulse in my mind. There's a lineup of faces that shuffle past, though the only one I recognize is Zeke's flashing somewhere near the middle. I see the swamp, but there are no gravestones in the clearing. And then an unfamiliar house swims to the forefront, a large, boxy building sagging toward the mire on the same foundation as the one I had built.

These thoughts belong to Amos, I realize.

But the demon's walked this swamp for the last time.

The portal hungrily devours Amos's soul. I don't know if it's dead, or if it's just been sent back to hell. Honestly, I'd prefer that I never find out.

I don't fight as the spectral opening beckons me deeper. I'd made a deal with the devil. My soul has been forfeited since the very moment I first allowed Amos in.

Resigned, I prepare to meet my fate.

Jake!

The familiar voice jolts me from my complacency. For the first time since leaving my body, I glance around, searching for the source.

An otherworldly sight greets me.

Everything is awash with an unnatural red haze. The fuzzy outline of a man floats beside me. High above, I catch sight of a body–*my* body—drifting loosely in the mud. Panic slices through me as the scene threatens to drive me mad.

Jake!

The shape next to me once again demands my attention. There's something familiar about him, and I realize with a start that this must be the soul that fought Amos for control over my body.

This is Zeke.

There's very little time.

The foreign thought runs through my mind, and I recognize that it belongs to the ghost. The words are the understatement of the year. I'm literally being dragged down into hell. What more can this guy want? Why is he even here? To taunt me?

I'm here for Julia. She wouldn't want you to die alone.

Julia. Of course.

Even now, I can still feel the echoes of his feelings for my wife. The juxtaposition of his love against my hatred stirs a deep well of shame in me.

I should have cherished Julia when I had the chance. She's a beautiful, kind, intelligent woman. I was so focused on myself that I lost sight of what was standing right in front of me. All of the cheating, all of the lies—they were only ever a reflection of myself.

I dragged Julia, an innocent, into all of this. She never wanted to come out here to this horrible place. In fact, she'd hated the swamp since we first toured the property, and I'd be lying if I didn't admit that I bought the land simply because I wanted her to suffer a little.

And the deal with Amos was entirely my doing. My greed and avarice twisted me into something I could no longer recognize.

Even after drinking the potion so that Julia could be saved, I'm never going to be free of my transgressions. Repenting now is too little, too late.

But maybe it's time to do something not for my own redemption, but for Julia.

Something selfless.

I have no idea how to communicate without a body, but I do my best. I focus on my intentions and string the words together clearly through my mind before projecting them over to the figure of Zeke.

The shape's head tilts, listening. I'm not sure if what I'm suggesting is even possible, but I have to keep up hope that maybe, just maybe, I can do this one last thing for Julia.

Are you sure?

I can sense Zeke's hesitation in his response.

I'm absolutely sure. In fact, I've never been so certain of anything in my entire life.

Thank you.

Zeke's gratitude flows through me, and I know that I've made the right choice.

I fight against the current of the portal for a moment longer. I need to make sure that Zeke does what I've asked. True to his word, his amorphous spirit surges upward through the mud, moving swiftly toward the prone shape of my body. He disappears into the torso, and for one tense moment, nothing happens.

But then, one of the arms twitches, and I know that it's worked.

My last act of love is complete.

The void beneath me changes from that red glow to a soft yellow light, and I think maybe I have redeemed myself after all.

It's time for me to go, and I'm not afraid.

28
THROUGH HIS EYES

Zeke

I'VE BEEN GIVEN A TREMENDOUS GIFT.

I hover for a moment next to the vacant body that floats limply in the mud and glance down at the harrowing scene below.

The ghoulish red glow emanating from the gaping maw of the portal illuminates the tableau, though I see a soft white light as well. Jake's soul, now cleaved from his flesh, is dragged ever downward into the abyss in Amos's wake, but I'm hopeful that change in the light means his last act redeemed him enough to save his soul.

As much as I despise Jake for having harmed Julia so deeply, I'm also filled with a grudging sense of respect for the dying wish he imparted onto me. I have no doubt that he understands that he wasn't capable of coming back and living a life that would make up for all he has done. Offering me his body wasn't for him, not one bit.

This is for Julia, a final act of the love that once flared between them.

I'll do my best to honor Jake's last request.

But can it even be done?

I've never heard of a spirit inhabiting a body that's already lost its soul. I don't even know if it's possible. But at the same time, haven't I already experienced the impossible? After dying at the malicious hand of a demon, I was condemned to walk this property as a mere shade of myself. Who am I to say this won't work?

Bolstered by this hope, I picture Julia's glowing face in my mind.

I have to try for her.

I reach out toward the lifeless body, copying how I jumped Jake earlier today.

Please let this work.

Every ounce of my very being calls out to the universe as I fill the void Jake left behind.

The experience of possessing the body is different this time. There's no squeezing push against the bulk of Jake's consciousness, nor the rend of Amos's sharpened mind against my own. There's nobody here to fight me, to push me out.

I simply slide into the vessel, peacefully, and with no resistance.

Sensations hit me all at once. Whereas my experiences had previously been muted by the presence of Jake's primary hold over this body, I'm now bearing the whole breadth of that feeling, of having a heart that beats and blood that pumps. It's clear that Jake's body isn't working at first, but with my burst of energy, things begin to drastically change inside of this corpse.

The most urgent thing is the burn of my lungs. It takes everything in me not to take a reflexive breath. It would certainly be a harsh fate to finally have a body again after almost a century only to immediately drown in the muck of the swamp.

I'm aware of my limbs next, and I flex them experimentally. The motions are clumsy and uncoordinated, but I suppose that's to be expected after not having a flesh and blood vessel for the last hundred years. I'm bound to be a little out of practice.

Satisfied that I'm in control, I glance down for a final glimpse of the waring lights below.

Jake's spirit gazes up at me for one last time.

I offer him a nod, but I'm not sure if he sees it.

A split second later, he slips soundlessly into the void, gone forever.

The portal pulses once, and then collapses in on itself, leaving me in darkness once again.

The need for air is painful now, searing through my chest. Acting more on instinct than intent, I move my limbs, steering myself upward. With the light gone, I'm trapped in thick, directionless darkness. I can only hope that I'm moving toward the surface.

It feels like an eternity passes before one hand rushes through the resistance of the mud and into the air. Black spots dance in my vision as I claw my way toward the surface, struggling to find purchase in the slick muck.

Hands grasp my arms, fingers digging into my skin as somebody hauls me forward in a series of sharp yanks.

Finally, my head breaches the slime.

Immediately, I gasp for air. The stench of the swamp floods my mouth and nose, but it's still the sweetest I've ever tasted. It smells of death and rebirth, of loss and of life.

Of new beginnings fashioned from the past.

"Jake! Jake, can you hear me?"

The voice swims to my awareness as though from underwater. It takes me a moment to realize that the speaker is talking to me.

I raise a hand to my face in an attempt to smear the mud from my eyes. It doesn't take me long to realize that's a futile task, given that I'm covered in the stuff.

"Let me," the familiar voice insists. As fabric runs over my face, I become more aware of myself.

I'm lying on my back, presumably in the clearing where my bones had once rested. My head throbs dully, and my neck is plagued by a deep ache. My body feels heavy, as though the mud has leached my muscles of all their energy.

"Jake?" It's Julia's voice, but she doesn't sound too enthusiastic about having her husband back. I can't really blame her, not after everything he'd done. She clearly doesn't realize it's me yet, but part of me is afraid that she'll never believe that I am who I say I am. Wouldn't that be a cruel fate for the both of us?

It takes a colossal amount of effort to peel my eyelids apart. When I do, Julia gasps in surprise.

"Zeke?" she exclaims in shock.

Her face swims into view, hazy at first before wavering into focus. Like me, she's covered in mud. Her auburn tresses are stained brown and hang limply around her shoulders. Blood, partially dried, cakes her hairline. But the light in her emerald eyes is still there.

Amos was unable to break her after all.

I open my mouth and test out my new voice. "It's me," I rasp. It's so strange to hear my words through the tones of another man, but I'll get used to it. I'm just grateful to have a body again.

Julia's eyes glisten with relieved tears that glimmer in the moonlight. "Oh my God," she breathes reverently. "It really is you!"

Even though I'm overjoyed that she has no doubts about my identity, I murmur, "How did you know?"

She offers me a brilliant smile. "Your eyes," she says. "I would recognize your eyes anywhere." Her fingers trace lightly over my cheekbone and come to frame my face. I lean into her tender touch. My heart aches with joy as she leans down to press her lips gently against mine.

I wish we could stay here forever, cloaked in this sweet moment, but we both know that we've got a lifetime of love to look forward to, and so Julia eventually pulls back with a soft, apologetic smile.

It's only then that I realize we're not alone here in the clearing.

An older woman with graying hair steps forward into view. She looks familiar, and it takes me a moment to recognize her as Julia's neighbor, Helen.

"You must be Zeke," she says, as though my habitation of Jake's body is the most normal thing in this world.

I nod stiffly.

"Is it done?" she probes. "Is Amos dead?"

I nod again, but Helen isn't satisfied with that answer.

"You're absolutely sure?" Her gaze is hard but haunted, and I wonder just how much Amos has terrorized her over the years as the closest neighbor to the old Gregory place.

"I saw it," I confirm. "It's gone."

Helen's shoulders sag in relief. "Thank God," she murmurs.

"What about Jake?" Julia's tone is tinged with guilt as she finds my hand with her own. I lace my fingers through hers and offer a reassuring squeeze.

"I'm sorry," I whisper.

Tears once again well in Julia's eyes at the news. Even though she must have already come to that conclusion, I understand that she just needed the confirmation. Grief sets across the planes of her delicate features.

"I need to know more," she insists.

I open my mouth to fulfill her request, but Helen cuts me off. "Honey, there will be plenty of time to talk about what happened, but both of you are a mess. Let's get inside, clean you up, patch up what we can, and have a hot drink."

Julia glances down at herself, as though realizing for the first time how grimy she is. After a moment, she nods wearily.

"Can you stand?" she asks me.

"I think so," I reply, though I'm truly not entirely sure.

In the end, it takes both Julia and Helen to help me to my feet. My legs wobble underneath me, but I'm stable enough with the two women propping me up.

Together, we hobble through the dredged remains of the swamp and back toward the house. The darkened building, once bustling with the souls of the dead, is empty now, hollow.

Perhaps Julia and I can fill the space with life again.

The thought gives me the strength to traverse the rest of the journey to the back porch. Helen instructs us to clean up while she puts some tea on, and we dutifully obey. While Julia retreats to the master bedroom, I shower in one of the guest rooms. The wound in my head has stopped bleeding, though the hot water makes it sting. I dab it dry before throwing on some of Jake's clothes. It feels odd to dress in a stranger's garments, just one more thing I'll have to adjust to.

We all meet again in the kitchen where Helen is waiting with two steaming mugs.

"You're not staying?" Julia asks.

Helen shakes her head. "I have a feeling that you two have a lot to discuss," she replies. "But I'll be just next door if you need me."

She catches Julia in a warm hug before reaching her arms out to me. I embrace her gladly. I'll forever be in her debt for the part she played in banishing Amos.

Julia and I don't speak until we hear the rumble of Helen's car in the driveway. In that silent space, I let my gaze run over the form of the woman I love.

She's once again wearing a dress, this one a pale cream color, along with a matching pair of heels. Her hair, damp from the shower, is still the lustrous auburn I remember. She's even taken the time to brush on some light makeup. It doesn't hide the bruises on her cheek, though. Seeing her so put together after everything she's been through, I can't help but feel that this is a sign that we're going to be okay.

Eventually, Julia speaks. "Did he suffer?" Her voice is small, guilty.

"Not at the end," I reassure her.

She regards me with wide, surprised eyes. "You were there?"

"Until he was gone," I confirm. "I knew you wouldn't want him to be alone."

Fresh tears course down Julia's cheeks at my words. Her hand finds mine, her palm warm against my skin. "Thank you." She squeezes her eyes closed. "He died because of me."

I shake my head. "He died because he made bad choices." I push back gently. "He understood that at the end. That's why he let me have his body. He didn't want you to be alone. He wanted to be happy." I don't think Jake was strong enough to force his way back into his dead body and make his heart beat again, but I was, and that strength came from my love for Julia.

A sob of mingled grief and relief escapes her mouth. I wrap my arms around her as she presses her face into my chest. It doesn't escape my notice that this is where I first held Julia all those weeks ago. It feels fitting, somehow, that we're here at this moment.

Although Jake's path has ended, ours is just beginning.

Amos is gone. Julia is free of both of her tormentors. And I've got a real, flesh and blood body.

We have a chance now to build a life together from the ashes of what we lost.

I press a kiss to the crown of Julia's head and gather her more securely in my embrace, feeling more alive than I've ever been.

29

· YOURS FOR ETERNITY

Julia

The whole house feels different now.

For the first time since moving here, I'm not plagued by the sensation of being watched. No more creaks or bangs plague the endless rooms. The laughter and running footsteps of ghostly children no longer echo through the halls. All of the noises I attributed to the settling of new construction are gone.

It's quiet now.

Empty.

"They've all moved on," Zeke explains when I ask if he notices it too. "They gave everything to help defeat Amos."

"Moved on?" I repeat, morbidly curious. "To where?"

Zeke shrugs. "Heaven, I guess. Or maybe another dimension. I don't really know for sure. I suppose if there were bad ones, they got sucked down into the portal with Amos."

It strikes me that these spirits must have become family to Zeke over the last century that he's walked this land. Even the annoying or unpleasant ones must have grown on him.

"Do you miss them?" I ask gently.

The glimmer of sadness in Zeke's honeyed eyes confirms my suspicions. "I do," he says in a soft voice. "Miss Penny most of all. I used to spend time by her beside when she was still alive. Everyone thought she was crazy, talking to thin air, but really, I just wanted her to know that somebody was looking out for her."

He falls silent, lost in the memory. I take the opportunity to study him. It's a little weird to look at Jake's body knowing that my husband is gone, but I believe I'll get used to it over time. Maybe someday, the warmth of the final sacrifices Jake made for me will replace the grief of losing him. Until then, I'll just continue being thankful for the opportunity to be with the man I truly love.

After all, I never let myself believe that Zeke and I could ever find a way to be together, not completely. But now, he sits beside me at the kitchen island, flesh and blood. I know we won't waste this opportunity.

My mind creeps back to Jake. He did so many terrible things. I'm already horribly aware of the cheating and the violence. I suspect that his business dealings were not of the ethical variety. Now, Zeke will have to clean all of that up.

And then there's the matter of Amos.

In spite of Jake's sacrifice and selfless last request for Zeke to inhabit his body, my husband handed me over to Amos with little resistance. While I'm still not sure how much of Jake's abuse was due to the demon's influence, I know that Jake was an active participant in much of it.

Does that mean he deserved to die?

I have a feeling that this question will haunt me for a very long time.

"Hey." Zeke catches my gaze, concern etched into his features. Though his body is unmistakably Jake's, his eyes are the warm honey hue I've come to associate with him. "Are you okay?"

I offer him a wry smile. "Ask me again tomorrow."

"I'm just glad there will be a tomorrow," Zeke replies. "It feels unreal that Amos is finally gone."

"It does," I agree. "I actually felt it when it died. It was like the whole swamp was different somehow. Like the land itself knew."

"Speaking of the swamp, we both absolutely reek," he comments lightly. I know he's trying to cheer me up, and I give in to it gratefully.

"Are you trying to tell me I smell?" I gasp in feigned offense.

"I'm trying to tell you that you need another shower," Zeke counters. He pauses for a moment before adding, "I could use one too."

My eyebrows draw upward at the implication. He meets my questions with a strong, certain gaze.

Wordlessly, I take his hand and tug, urging him to stand. He does so dutifully and trails behind me as I guide him out of the kitchen, down the hallway, and up the stairs.

The lighter mood shifts in intensity as we step into the master bedroom. Zeke's eyes grow hot with desire, and I know I'm regarding him just as hungrily.

It's me who makes the first move.

Moving slowly so he doesn't miss a single thing, I slide the thin straps of my dress over my shoulders. No longer secured, the loose dress ripples easily down my body to pool at my feet.

Zeke's eyes widen at the sight of me standing before him in only my lingerie. If the growing bulge in his pants is anything to go by, I think it's safe to say that he likes what he sees.

I turn around and glance over my shoulder coyly as I reach around to unhook my bra. The lacy garment falls to join the dress on the carpet. From there, I bend over. Zeke sucks in an audible breath at the sight. I very purposely take my time removing one heel, and then the other, before straightening up again.

Finally, I turn back around to face the man I love.

Desire paints his features, but there's a reverence there too as his eyes pass over every inch of me, as though committing my form to memory. I feel like a goddess under his gaze.

"Beautiful," he murmurs.

Emboldened by his response, I slide my thong down my long legs and stand bare in front him. Before he can make a move, I stride confidently past him to the bathroom. I pause on the threshold and spare him a glance.

"Aren't you going to join me?" I beckon.

I can hear Zeke shedding his clothes as I start the shower and step under the spray of the water. I stand with my back toward the sliding door, eagerly awaiting my lover's arrival.

The sound of the shower door almost makes me jump with anticipation. Zeke's hands immediately come to rest on my hips as he pulls me flush against his chest. The evidence of his desire is heavy against the small of my back, and I instantly feel a rush of wet heat between my legs.

Zeke's lips fan gentle kisses over my hair and down toward the soft skin of my neck. I lean my head to the side, allowing him better access. At the same time, his hands skim up my sides to caress the soft swell of my breasts.

A breathy gasp escapes me as his fingers trace the tender peaks of my nipples. Zeke's hips buck at the sound. I can only imagine what this must feel like for him after not having a physical body for so long, though there was that one night we shared together with him in Jake's body.

While one hand continues to tease the sensitive skin of my breasts, the other trails on a southern path toward the juncture of my thighs. He skims over my belly before dipping his fingers lower to ghost over my core. I shiver in anticipation as he continues to circle my slick heat.

Just when I think I'll go mad with desire, he slides one finger inside.

I moan at the sudden intrusion.

"You're already so wet for me," Zeke marvels as he gently pumps his finger through my slick folds. "I can feel how much you want me."

"I do," I gasp as I rock my hips, seeking more friction. "Please, Zeke, I want you."

As though he's rewarding me, his thumb brushes against my clit.

"Please," I whine as I rock against his hand. "More."

Zeke, ever the gentleman, obliges.

He quickens the rhythm, giving me more of what I crave. Sensing that it's still not enough, he adds another finger, stretching me deliciously. As he presses into me, his thumb provides my clit with some much needed attention.

I'm a dripping mess under his ministrations. My legs shudder beneath me as he brings me closer and closer to the edge.

"Come for me, Julia," he whispers in my ear. "I want to feel you."

I come undone at his words, spasming on his fingers. A wanton moan floats from my lips as pleasure jolts through me. I realize dimly that Jake never made me come like this. Only Zeke has only ever drawn this sort of ecstasy out of me.

Now, I want to show him the same sort of heaven.

I turn in Zeke's grasp, relishing the feeling of his hard length trailing against my skin. His honeyed eyes track my movements with hot intensity as I kneel before him until I'm level with his cock.

My hands slide up his muscled thighs as I take the tip of him in my mouth.

"Julia," he gasps as my lips close over the silky skin of his shaft. His hands twine through my hair, but he's gentle in his grasp.

Empowered by his desire, I begin to work my mouth over him, taking in as much of his cock as I can manage. I close one hand over the base of his shaft and massage him while my tongue does the rest.

The groans my efforts elicit from him are sweeter than honey. Part of me longs to take him over the edge like this. Only the thought of his cock sliding deep into my dripping pussy stops me.

Zeke seems to have the same idea. His hands frame my face, guiding me off him and up to standing. He wastes no time in moving me until my back is against the smooth tile.

I wrap my arms around his shoulders as he ducks down to capture my lips in a heated kiss. I pour all of my love, all of my desire back into it.

Zeke pulls back, and for a split second, I'm worried that he's changed his mind now that he has a flesh and blood body. After all, I was never enough for Jake. He took every opportunity to cheat on me. Even though I know that Zeke is a far better man than my husband ever was, a small part of me fears that Zeke might eventually tire of me too.

Maybe he already has.

But the words he utters next send all of those doubts flying.

"I love you," he breathes.

Time seems to stop as the full force of his statement sinks in. When I'm finally ready to reply, my eyes are brimming with unshed tears.

"And I love you, Zeke," I murmur.

He once again catches me in a breathless kiss as his arms snake around me. He lifts me easily, and I wrap my legs around his waist. The head of his cock brushes against my entrance, causing me to moan against his mouth.

I let go of him for a moment to guide his length to my entrance. At the same time, I break the kiss only to catch his earlobe in my teeth, earning a delighted sigh from his lips.

"Show me," I whisper. "Make love to me."

His hips roll lazily, pushing his length into me. I moan into his neck at the sensation. Spurred on by my pleasure, Zeke starts up a slow, rhythmic pace. Every thrust guides his cock deeper into my tight pussy, filling me completely.

It doesn't take long before I'm once again overwhelmed with sensation. I squirm against him as he lowers me over and over again onto his dick, fanning the flames that are building inside of me.

And then I crest the peak, my mouth opening in a silent cry as the wave of pleasure breaks.

My inner walls flutter over Zeke's cock, driving him over the edge. He comes with a deep groan as he releases his essence inside of me.

We stay like that for a moment, him cradling me against him as his seed drips down my thighs.

Eventually, he pulls away, just far enough so that he can rest his forehead against mine.

"I love you, Julia," he says earnestly. "I promise I'll always take care of you. If you'll have me, I will give you all that I am. I'm yours, in death and in life."

His eyes meet mine, and I have no doubt that he's telling the truth.

Zeke is mine.

In death—and in life.

30

THE HOME AT THE EDGE OF THE SWAMP

JULIA

It's hard to believe that a whole year has passed since peace came to the house at the edge of the swamp.

I roll over in bed, blinking lazily in the golden sunlight that filters in through the windows. Zeke, already awake beside me, smiles.

"Good morning, beautiful." He greets me in a voice that's husky with sleep. He scoots closer to press a kiss to my lips.

It's chaste at first. But as the grogginess of slumber flows from my veins, the warmth of his body against mine starts to become awfully distracting. A stirring between Zeke's legs shows me that he's no more immune to our current situation than I am.

The kiss deepens as Zeke rolls on top of me, caging me in against the mattress. His body is deliciously firm against mine. No matter how many times we do this, I can never seem to get enough of him.

"You're insatiable," he murmurs against my lips.

"Only for you," I counter.

Can he really blame me? After so many years trapped with Jake as my partner, I didn't exactly get a chance to satisfy all of my carnal urges. I still have so much lost time to make up for. It's a good thing that Zeke is more than willing to help.

Zeke's lips travel lower, dipping to the slender curve of my neck before teasing the spot where the top of my nightgown meets the swell of my breasts. I squirm beneath him and roll my hips in a silent plea.

A warm chuckle rolls from his lips. "All in good time, sweetheart," he says playfully as his hands skim the hem of my nightgown.

I growl in frustration as his mouth travels down the fabric of my sleepwear. The sensation of the layers shifting against my heated skin is a tantalizing preview of what's to come.

Zeke tosses the sheets off me, exposing my slender legs to the morning air. His fingers brush the hem of my nightdress up higher, revealing the sheer thong underneath. The fabric is already damp with the evidence of my desire. It's a fact that doesn't go unnoticed by Zeke, who hums in approval at the sight.

"I love that you're always ready for me," he marvels as I tilt my legs open to give him a better view.

Beckoned in by my wanton action, Zeke hooks his fingers over the edge of my panties and slides them down my legs in one swift motion. A thrill of desire rushes through me as his warm breath puffs over my most sensitive area.

Zeke's eyes meet mine as he draws closer to my core. His gaze is aflame with want. He doesn't look away as his tongue darts out to taste me.

"Zeke!" I moan.

I can feel him grin against me as he licks me again before pulling away slightly. His eyes sparkle with the impish delight of a man who knows exactly what he's doing. It's the sweetest kind of torture.

"More," I plead. "Please, Zeke!"

There's a split second where he's still, and then his head dips forward to give me the attention I so badly need.

His tongue is everywhere. It circles my clit, dredging up a low moan from my throat, before exploring my slick entrance. My hips tilt to meet Zeke's mouth as he presses into me, and in response, he splays a strong hand against my taut stomach to keep me from moving too much.

Just as I'm getting used to the feeling of his mouth on me, he draws back. I whimper from the loss, but the sensation of his tongue is quickly replaced by one swirling finger.

I sigh as he buries the digit in my core. He growls in approval when I welcome him in greedily. It doesn't take long until he eases another finger inside of me. After a few languid pumps of his hand, he leans back down and closes his mouth over my clit.

An ecstatic cry tumbles from my lips. The mix of sensations is maddening. I mumble incoherent pleas into the morning air as Zeke expertly guides me closer and closer to my release.

As soon as I'm about to shatter, Zeke pulls away.

"Not yet, sweetheart," he murmurs as he stalks back up my body. "I want to watch you come undone on my cock."

I can think of nothing better.

As a promise of what's to come, he runs his length through my folds, collecting my essence on himself. After several teasing seconds, he finally lines his hips up with mine.

With one long, slow movement, he presses his cock into me. He doesn't stop until he's nestled completely in my hot pussy, lost within me.

He gives me a moment to adjust to the size of him, and then he starts to move. He pulls out until just the tip of his shaft remains inside of me before dragging all the way back in.

Pleasure flares within me as he continues his slow and tortuous rhythm. Soon, I'm writhing beneath him, my hips bucking up in an attempt to quicken his thrusts.

Watching my frustration grow, Zeke lets out a low laugh. "Am I going too slow for you?" he teases.

I nod vigorously even as he fills me with his cock once more.

"Then how about you set the pace?" he suggests.

In one smooth motion, he rolls us over so that he's now lying on his back with me straddling his hips. His dick is still sheathed deep inside of me, and the new angle leaves me breathless.

He doesn't have to ask me twice. I raise my hips until he's just barely contained within my wet heat before I sink back down onto him. Zeke groans as I repeat the process, quickening my rhythm until I'm bouncing on his cock.

One of his hands slides up to my breast. He rolls my nipple between his fingers, causing my hips to stutter. The other travels down toward where our bodies meet to find my clit. He traces lazy circles over the bundle of nerves. The combination of sensations is transcendent.

My body arches as I approach my oncoming release. Zeke can feel it too. His hands abandon their tasks to secure my hips, urging me to quicken my pace.

He comes first, emptying himself into me as I sink once more onto his cock. The sensation of his essence inside of me pushes me past the precipice toward my own undoing.

I let out a wild cry as the orgasm surges through me, and then I fall, spent and boneless, onto Zeke's chest.

Our blissful moment doesn't last long.

The baby monitor on the bedside table crackles to life, transmitting a sniffling sob into the room.

"Shit," I say, rolling off of Zeke. "I think we woke the baby."

Zeke laughs. "We're lucky we didn't wake Helen and Robert, to be honest," he counters. He sits up, already swinging his legs around to get out of bed. "I'll go."

"No, it's fine," I sigh. I take a brief moment in the bathroom to clean myself up before pulling my robe on and padding across the hall to the nursery.

Baby Penny, upon seeing me appear in the doorway, immediately stops fussing. She reaches for me with one small hand and smiles.

"Hello, Miss Penny," I coo as I scoop her out of her crib. "Did Mommy and Daddy wake you up?"

I rock her gently in my arms, marveling at our little miracle. She's only three months old, but she already looks a lot like me. Her fine hair matches my auburn shade, and she shares my dainty bone structure.

But those warn honey eyes? She inherited those from her dad.

Zeke, now wearing sweatpants and a T-shirt, joins me in the nursery. "How is my baby girl?" He takes Penny from me, cradling her gently in his strong arms. The sight never fails to make my heart burst with love and gratitude.

One year ago, I was so sure that there was no hope. I thought I'd be stuck in an abusive marriage with a demon hanging over my head forever, all while the man who would later capture my heart walked the property as a ghost.

I never would have imagined that I would be standing here today with Zeke and our perfect baby girl, our miracle family.

As Zeke rocks Penny in his arms, I catch a glimpse of him in the mirror. For a moment, I could swear that he looks like he did when I first met him, tall blond, chiseled, heartland charm. But the moment passes, and his face is Jake's once again.

I smile softly at the scene.

For all the challenges of inhabiting somebody else's body, Zeke adjusted to this new life surprisingly well. He stepped into Jake's business dealings almost immediately. It didn't take long for him to discover all the shady happenings lurking behind many of the business deals. He dealt with those swiftly and decisively, going so far as to report Jake's former associate Thurman for human trafficking.

Now, under Zeke's wise guidance, the companies are thriving. He even recently surprised me with a beautiful apartment in New York City, which we visit often.

"Julia, look," Zeke whispers, drawing me back to the scene before me. I peer over his arms to find Penny sleeping soundly against his chest.

"She's perfect," I breathe.

"Just like her mother," he grins. Taking great care not to wake her, Zeke lowers Penny gingerly back into the crib.

Once she's settled, we both tiptoe out of the room.

We end up in the kitchen, drinking coffee while we keep one ear on the baby monitor. Zeke ducks out for a moment to retrieve the newspaper from the driveway, leaving me in the peaceful golden light of the kitchen.

My mind drifts back to Amos. For the first few months after sending it back to hell, I was extremely jumpy. I expected it to come roiling back out of the swamp at any second, ready to exact revenge on Zeke and me.

But that day never came. The sun rises every morning over the marsh and then sets without incident. Even so, we never spend much time out there. I still hate the place, and Zeke is sick of it after so many ghostly years spent trapped in the mire.

I think about all of the weird stuff that happened that I since realized was the demon's doing. We haven't had any strange incidents since that day in the swamp. And I've never heard that creepy song again.

As if on cue, the speaker on the counter bursts to life.

I nearly jump out of my seat as a slow blues melody floods the kitchen, turning my blood to ice in my veins.

"Sweetheart, are you okay?" Zeke asks.

I whip around to find him in the doorway of the kitchen. He's got his phone in his hand, the screen illuminated with the bright colors of a playlist.

At the same time, the lyrics on the song start. A woman's voice laments through the speakers.

It's not the same song, not even close.

"I'm fine," I say sheepishly. I feel stupid for having panicked at such a small thing.

Zeke places his phone down on the kitchen island and wraps his arms around me. He begins to sway me back and forth in time with the beat.

I melt in his arms, my fear leaving me as swiftly as it came.

We stand in the middle of the kitchen, rocking one another to the tune from Zeke's youth. Golden sunlight filters in the windows around us, driving out any shadows that dare to linger. Upstairs, our baby girl sleeps peacefully.

This is the life I've always wanted.

I stand on my tiptoes and press my lips to Zeke's in a tender kiss. His arms tighten around me, drawing me closer.

And there, in the house at the edge of the swamp, the ghosts of our past are finally put to rest.

Mated to Four Alphas

Threats Against the Breeder

At War for the Breeder

The Stolen Breeder

Four Alphas, Four Babies

Becoming the Luna Queen

Descendants of the Breeder

Desired by the Devil series

Whispers of the Devil

Banter of the Devil

Murmurs of the Devil

The Mafia Kings series

Indebted to the Mafia King

Loved by the Mafia King

Claimed by the Mafia King

Secrets of the Mafia King

Burned by the Mafia King

Kidnapped by the Mafia King (coming soon!)

Dark Stalker Romance series

Tempted by Sin

Fated to Sin

Secret Billionaires series

Finding the Secret Billionaire by Olivia Bhelle Kildare

Falling for My Secret Billionaire by Bella Moondragon

Driven by the Secret Billionaire by ID Johnson

Wolf Shifter Alpha Kings series

Ravens and Ruins

Sundrops and Shadows

Snowflakes and Sabotage

The Vampire King's Feeder series

Claiming the Alpha's Daughter

Loving the Alpha's Daughter

Finding the Alpha's Daughter

Bewitching the Alpha's Son (coming soon!)

Writing as B. Moon

The Boy Who Died

Sign up for Bella's newsletter here.

Or get a free novella from The Alpha King's Breeder series when you sign up here: The Beta and the Maid

Follow Bella on Facebook here.

Follow Bella on Bookbub here.